Dragonfall 5
and the H

BRIAN

The ancient st
are hired to ta
Home, one of
So starts the
inhabited by
ride across the
Sanchez find t
with haunted
existence of I

DRAGONFALL 5
And the hunted
world By BRIAN
EARNSHAW

BIG MOTHER

OLD ELIAS

TIM & MINIMS

SANCHEZ & JERK

BRIAN EARNSHAW

Dragonfall 5 and the Haunted World

Illustrated by Simon Stern

A Magnet Book

Other Dragonfall 5 books by Brian Earnshaw:

DRAGONFALL 5 AND THE ROYAL BEAST
DRAGONFALL 5 AND THE EMPTY PLANET
DRAGONFALL 5 AND THE HIJACKERS
DRAGONFALL 5 AND THE SPACE COWBOYS
DRAGONFALL 5 AND THE MASTER MIND
DRAGONFALL 5 AND THE SUPER HORSE

First published in Great Britain 1979
by Methuen Children's Books Ltd
Magnet paperback edition first published 1983
by Methuen Children's Books Ltd
11 New Fetter Lane, London EC4P 4EE
Text copyright © 1979 Brian Earnshaw
Illustrations copyright © 1979
Methuen Children's Books Ltd
Printed in Great Britain by
Cox & Wyman Ltd, Reading

ISBN 0 416 30090 1

Chapter 1

After three weeks in the mists of hyperspace *Dragon-fall 5* was coasting down under rocket power through clear air in the silver sunlight of the mega-strength star, Khosro Khai. Below them Pine Home, the larger of the twin planets that circled Khosro Khai, loomed dark and green. Pine Home was so close now that Sanchez could see a white city between a forest and a lake. Far out in the sky, across a million miles of space, the second planet, the one called Lost Home, shone tawny gold with its deserts. But as the old starship came blasting down to cloud level Sanchez and his brother Tim, who was piloting, only had eyes for one thing.

'Elephants flying!' called Sanchez happily. 'Loads of them!'

'Not really flying.' Tim liked to be accurate.

'The next best thing,' Sanchez insisted, 'they've got hang gliders with rocket boosters. Lucky them! Perhaps we can have a try on them when we've landed and we've got some money again.'

'You'll have to ask your father.' Big Mother was pretending to knit but really she was keeping an eye on Tim's piloting as they made their landing approach.

Old Elias, their father, was at his work bench re-writing the log book of their voyage. He had got them lost twice in hyperspace and now he was faking the records to make it look as if they had just been taking things easily. *Dragonfall 5* was more than sixty years old, a vintage starship, so the authorities were always trying to cancel their star licence and put *Dragonfall* in a museum. Because of this Old Elias liked to keep the records looking efficient, even if they were not really so.

He grunted over his papers: 'Hang gliders are a fool enough way of getting around without adding rocket boosters. Trust elephants to think of some nonsense.'

As he looked up from his log his eyes widened. 'Watch out, boy! Hard astern!' he shouted.

But even as his father spoke, Tim acted, slamming on *Dragonfall*'s anti-gravity field and her reverse rocket drive at one and the same time to bring the ship to a dead halt. He was just in time to avoid a large red hang glider which had swung round in an air current and now went wobbling across their path only a few yards from their needle-sharp nose cone. Hanging from the glider was a small elephant in a smart black flying outfit. He waved his trunk cheerfully at the crew and was gone out of sight to their left.

'Steam gives way to sail,' said Old Elias. 'Always remember that. We're in control and they're not.'

'Was that a baby elephant?' Sanchez asked in surprise. 'It was no bigger than me.'

'No, they don't grow any bigger on Pine Home,' Old Elias answered. 'That one was full grown. They're as nippy on their feet as you are.'

'And it seemed to be covered in short blond fur,' Sanchez added, 'or was it a mask? Let's get near to another one and see.'

'Tim will give hang gliders a wide berth if he's got any sense,' said Big Mother firmly. 'The way ahead's clear now. Let's get moving again slowly and fly clear of this crowd.'

All around the motionless starship hang gliders

8

were wheeling and turning in the sharp breeze at ten thousand feet. Red, white and black, they hung and swung on the currents, or shot forward on rocket boosters, leaving thick white smoke trails behind them.

Tim eased out of anti-gravity; the cups in the kitchen swung again and rattled. Gently he fired the rocket pod on the short cut-back wings and they continued carefully down on low power. The flock of hang gliders was soon left behind and Old Elias relaxed.

'It wasn't a mask,' he told the crew, 'all the elephants on this planet have got short blond fur and they wear clothes, leather gear mostly, on account of the cold climate.'

'So really,' said Sanchez, 'they're not elephants but very small mammoths. Like we used to have in the Ice Age on Earth.'

'Mini-mammoths!' Tim laughed. 'That's a great name!'

'Call them what you like up here,' said Big Mother, 'but you mind your manners when we get down there. Remember one of them is going to pay us fifty-six thousand credits when we deliver our cargo! They may be our size but they're much richer.'

'We really do need that money, don't we?' Sanchez sighed.

'We certainly do, boy,' his mother agreed. 'Three weeks in hyperspace has eaten up all our fuel and food. Of course we weren't expecting to be longer than two weeks on the journey.'

9

She looked accusingly at Old Elias who coughed and made a big fuss of lighting his pipe.

'But this is how it's worked out,' she continued, 'and, until we get paid, do you know what we're going to be eating?'

'Spaghetti?' Tim suggested.

'Right first time,' said Big Mother and settled back in her chair.

Sanchez groaned and Jerk, their Flying Hound Dog, made a sympathetic whimpering sound. It had been an easy guess. They had had nothing else to eat but spaghetti for the last three days.

'I tell you what,' said Old Elias. 'When we get down to Kantaroom City and I've signed for those fifty-six thousand credits I'll take you all to the best restaurant in the place and you can eat whatever you fancy.'

'Lovely food! Do you think we could fly a bit quicker?' Sanchez asked his brother hopefully.

'No need to make for the Space Port,' said Tim proudly. 'With our rocket engines we can drop right into the firm's back yard.'

That was true. *Dragonfall*'s one big advantage over modern starships was that she could land and take off anywhere she wanted. She might be slow, but she didn't need the big landing cradles that most modern ships depended on.

'What was the name of the firm again?' Sanchez asked. 'I love hearing it.'

Old Elias read from his papers, 'Keeson, Koolyson, Kossetson and King Limited.'

'It must be a very big firm with a name like that,' Sanchez said.

'Let's hope so,' said Big Mother gloomily. 'They've got a very big bill to pay us!'

'Kantaroom City ahead,' Tim called out. 'It's three miles off on that lake shore. We're down to five thousand feet. Where do I go?'

'South-east quarter of the city, grid reference 82 by 64,' Old Elias read out, 'and look for a park with a steep hill in the middle. The firm's warehouses are alongside the park.'

Dragonfall 5 swung in a splendid arc over a lake alive with sailing boats, then across a lakefront of tall white buildings with domes and towers. Losing height but still spouting fire from her rocket pods, she crossed a town of winding roads, low houses and gardens.

'Got it,' Tim called as he followed his father's map directions. 'Park, hill and warehouses. Permission to land?'

'Land away!' Old Elias replied.

The hum of anti-gravs surrounded them again. The blue and silver ship poised over a large yard surrounded by factory sheds and storehouses. Carefully, Tim brought her down on twin columns of whistling rocket exhaust. Dust whirled on the ground below, shed doors flapped and banged. With a tiny jolt they landed.

'Wow!' said Sanchez. 'After all these weeks Jerk'll be glad of a run, won't you, Jerk?' He rubbed the Flying Hound Dog's big silky black ears and unfastened the cabin door.

11

'Good landing, boy,' Old Elias nodded approvingly to Tim. Big Mother got up and put her knitting away. Fresh cool air floated into the cabin as Sanchez swung open the door and jumped down. It had been a very long crossing.

'Now let's find the cargo receiver,' said Big Mother, poking her head out and gazing around the yard. 'I don't mind whether he's Keeson, Koolyson, Kossetson or King so long as he pays cash on delivery!'

Sanchez was looking around the yard. It seemed very quiet and yet the shed doors all gaped wide open.

'I think it must be lunch time,' he said. 'There's no one about.'

'It's only three hours after sunrise, local time,' said Tim, jumping down to join his brother. 'Perhaps they get up late.'

Old Elias and Big Mother climbed down the ladder. The crew looked about them.

'Oh dear,' said Sanchez. 'I think something has gone wrong!'

All around the yard the empty windows and open doors looked back at them. There was not an elephant or a human in sight; no one had worked in this factory for weeks. A hover car hummed past in the street outside. *Dragonfall*'s rocket pods made clicking sounds as the metal cooled.

'There's a notice pasted up over that gate,' Big Mother nodded, 'and I think I know what it says, if only we could read the language.'

'Minims please,' Sanchez called up to the open cabin. 'Here's some work for you at last!'

12

With a sleepy chittering noise the three Minims woke on their perch, peeked out of the door, and then came swinging eagerly down to sit on Sanchez's shoulder. They loved work, and work for them was translating foreign languages into English. A cargo-carrying starship like *Dragonfall 5* was always calling at strange planets and running into language difficulties; so usually the Minims were busy and happy. It was only in hyperspace where there was nothing to do but eat spaghetti that they got bored and bad-tempered. They looked like grey furry chipmunks with pouchy throats and they always worked telepathically in teams of three. Usually the eldest of the three did most of the talking and the youngest did the least. Perhaps the best thing about Minims was that the more work they got the less wages they wanted because they just loved to be the centre of attention.

They preened their fur as Sanchez walked over to the notice.

'We'd like to know what this says,' Sanchez pointed.

'Telepathic contact with a notice is difficult,' said the first Minim.

'But we will do the best,' said the second.

'That we can,' finished the third, who was learning his trade and never got much that was important to say.

The Minims stared at the notice and *Dragonfall*'s crew waited anxiously. The white sun slid behind a cloud and suddenly the wind made them think of snow and sleet showers.

13

'This notice,' began the first Minim, clearing his throat, 'is to warn all traders that the firm of Keeson, Koolyson, Kossetson and King,'

'Electrical Engineers,' said the second.

'Is bankrupt!' the third Minim squeaked triumphantly. He had never had anything half as important to say before.

'Bankrupt?' gasped Sanchez.

'That means they've run out of money,' Tim explained.

'Gone broke!' added Old Elias.

'But we've carried a load of electronic tracking equipment halfway across the galaxy for them,' Sanchez cried. 'Three whole weeks in boring old hyperspace.'

'And the last three days of it on spaghetti,' Tim added.

'They owe us fifty-six thousand credits!' said Sanchez in despair.

'Which we are not going to get,' Big Mother said quietly, and she climbed back up into *Dragonfall*.

'Stuck on the outer edge of the universe without a penny to our name,' said Old Elias bitterly. 'I always said it was bad business to carry goods cash on delivery. Money first and service afterwards is my rule.'

He turned and climbed up after Big Mother.

Tim and Sanchez looked at each other. It was all very well for Old Elias to say 'money first and service afterwards'. They knew that cargoes were few and far between these days. The whole crew had been very happy to get this job of picking up a load of delicate electronic tracking gear from an asteroid in the Alpha Lictus belt and bringing it here to Pine Home for repair.

Now it had all gone wrong. Keeson, Koolyson, Kossetson and King, who were to do the repairs, had gone broke and *Dragonfall* was broke too. The sky darkened over their heads but they did not look up.

'Just what are we going to do?' Sanchez demanded.

'Are you asking that question to get an answer or just to let off steam?' a very educated voice called down from above them.

Jerk growled and the boys looked up. A blue hang glider was poised about ten feet above them, dipping and fluttering just near stalling point. As they watched, it dropped neatly down on to the yard and the elephant who had been flying it slipped out of his harness. He looked very pleased with himself.

'My sister is landing,' he said without explanation.

Overhead there was a flurry and flap of brilliant silver fabric as another hang glider swung in to land rather badly. The second elephant pilot was helped out of her harness by the first. Both wore blue suede flying suits with gold buttons. The sister elephant let her glider wing fall back on to the paving stones and ran her trunk carefully over her face to smooth down the sleek blond fur. Then she turned to the boys.

> '*Even in clouds of darkest night*
> *Hope is near and shines most bright,*'

she said, then looked dreamily away.

'My sister is a poet,' the first elephant explained cheerfully. 'What she means is that there is always something practical you can do, and if we can be of any help to the strangers who own such a beautiful old starship we will be delighted.'

'That's very kind of you,' said Tim politely.

'I will introduce us,' the first elephant continued firmly. 'I am Sigmond Sigson. This is my sister Morween Ildadaughter. We are students in our fourteenth year at Kantaroom University. I study law; my sister studies Intergalactic Poetry.'

'I'm Tim,' said Tim.

'And I'm Sanchez,' said Sanchez.

'We help our parents to run *Dragonfall 5*,' Tim pointed to their starship, 'though some day we'll have to go to university too.'

'But only for three years,' said Sanchez. 'Isn't fourteen years rather a long time to go on being a student?'

'There is so much to learn,' Sigmond replied airily, with a wave of his trunk. 'Here on Pine Home we take our time.'

'Time!' his sister turned as if they had said something important.

'Time is the golden treasure of the wise spirit,' she added solemnly.

There was a pause. The boys could see that Morween Ildadaughter was a full-time poet, but it was difficult to know how to treat her. Sanchez thought of something safe which he could ask.

'Excuse me,' he said, 'but if you are brother and sister, how is it that you have different surnames?'

'Our father,' explained Sigmond, 'is called Sigmond like me, so my name is Sigmond Sigson. Our mother is called Ilda so Morween is called Morween Ildadaughter. You see?'

'That's very sensible,' said Tim. 'It's fair to both sides.'

'We are a fair and sensible race,' Sigmond smiled. 'As a result we are rolling in money! Now tell us all your troubles and we'll solve them together.'

'How did you know we'd got troubles?' Tim asked doubtfully.

17

'Wasn't your brother complaining about them as we flew past a few minutes ago?' Sigmond answered smoothly.

Tim hesitated a second. It was all happening rather too neatly, but they really were in a fix and someone was going to have to help them. So he explained everything: their journey, the bankrupt firm and the money they could not collect. Sigmond listened carefully and Morween sighed in sympathy.

'Ah!' said Sigmond wisely. 'When you saw the name of the firm you might have guessed that they would go bankrupt.'

'How's that?' Sanchez asked.

'All elephant names end in '-son,' Sigmond explained. 'You have three elephants in the firm, Keeson, Koolyson and Kossetson, but only one human, Mr King. This is not a good combination. The best firms are half elephant and half human.'

'Why?' Tim was puzzled.

'We elephant people of Pine Home are a cheerful, noble race: poets, inventors, rulers. But when it comes to running a sound reliable business like electrical engineering it is best to rely on humans. Though they have their odd sense of humour, at heart they are gloomy so they work hard to forget their gloom. Human businesses do not often go bankrupt.'

'We didn't even know you had humans here,' said Sanchez. 'We thought you were all elephants.'

'Nine hundred years ago we were,' said Sigmond.

Morween began to chant in her poetic voice:

*'Out of the dark night of space a bird came burning,
Winged from a dying world it brought us human
learning.'*

'As my sister says,' Sigmond explained, 'the
humans used to live only on the twin planet, the one
we call Lost Home, but that began to turn into a
desert so they escaped in space ships and came to
us on Pine Home. This is the elephants' planet, but
we had plenty of water and plenty of room so
humans and elephants have lived happily together
ever since.'

'No quarrels?' Tim asked.

'Nothing serious,' said Sigmond. 'Humans have
their failings, but we elephants can deal with them
because we are practical and always hope for the
best.

'But now, enough of this pleasant chatter. A light
refreshing shower is beginning. Lead us to your
parents and we will tell them how to put all their
troubles right.'

In fact an icy downpour had begun with great
lumps of sleet. The two elephants scrambled easily
up the ladder and the boys showed them into the
control cabin.

'This is Sigmond and this is Morween,' Sanchez
introduced them. 'They say they can get us out of
trouble quite easily, so we've brought them up.'

Sigmond looked around eagerly.

'What magnificent craftsmanship!' he declared.
'What a beautiful old ship. It's like going round a
historical museum and it's all still working!'

Old Elias looked a little huffy about this, but Big Mother insisted on offering the visitors tea.

This led to difficulties.

'In this world of ours we do not use any kind of fire or heat to prepare our food and drink,' Sigmond explained. 'This tea of yours will give us great pleasure, but we will just stir the leaves in cold healthy water.'

'With sugar,' Big Mother suggested.

'Sugar is prepared with heat and boiling. Thank you, no.' Sigmond was polite but firm.

So *Dragonfall*'s crew sat swizzling tea leaves around in their cups with cold water, wondering how they could get out of drinking it. Old Elias was so nervous that he began to light his pipe, but when Sanchez pulled a face he remembered that lighting a pipe would use heat, so he stopped.

'To sit here is like taking a trip back in time,' said Sigmond, looking around appreciatively.

'We like it,' Big Mother replied. 'It's our home.'

Sigmond drained his tea cup in one swig and smacked his lips.

'An interesting drink,' he said. 'I see you have new foods to show us and many quaint customs. Your father even burns leaves in his face. This is good. Listen to what I propose. You need money. Right?'

'Right,' said Old Elias.

'Here on Pine Home we have money, we have much free time, we like to enjoy ourselves. Right?'

This time no one answered because no one could guess what was coming next.

'Most of all,' Sigmond continued, 'we like
20

antiques, beautiful old things like your starship. Look at her! Her fine lines, her ancient equipment, her lovely colours.'

'We wouldn't think of selling *Dragonfall*,' Sanchez protested.

'Naturally not,' Sigmond agreed. 'But rich folk from Pine Home will pay you good money to be taken for holiday tours in such a distinguished vessel. To go with your *Dragonfall* will be like a trip back into the past for them. You have rocket pods, galactic integrators, why, your craft even has wings! You could offer low-speed panoramic tours!'

Dragonfall's crew were not quite sure that they liked being part of a trip back into the past.

'There's no room for guests,' said Big Mother practically. 'You can see how we're crowded together here.' She nodded towards the hammocks in the back of the cabin, the perch for the Minims, Jerk's hanging basket. 'Do you want us to put the guests in the cargo hold?'

'Of course not,' Sigmond paused, smiling brilliantly. 'You will tow a luxurious caravan far behind you. Then your paying guests will have both the old and the new.'

'And how do we pay for the caravan?' asked Old Elias crossly. He knew just how much a caravan glider on a tow rope would slow *Dragonfall* down and he didn't like the idea.

'Sell this electronic equipment which you have brought.' Sigmond looked around waiting for congratulations. Slowly *Dragonfall*'s crew began to brighten up.

'That sounds like a very good idea,' said Big Mother.

'But is the tracking gear ours to sell?' Tim asked.

'Does anyone else claim it?' Sigmond asked reasonably.

'So *Dragonfall* would be going into the package tour business!' Sanchez thought it all sounded much more fun than another three weeks in the mists of hyperspace.

'Where would we take them on these tours?' Tim was always practical.

'There is only one place,' said Sigmond confidently. 'To Lost Home. That is where our humans go for all their holidays. It has ruined cities, lovely old houses, sunsets that last all day long, flaming with colour. Best of all it has the finest hang gliding in the galaxy. You can take your guests to ride the thunderstorms and whirlwinds of the Antovin mountains. There is no sport like it!'

'That sounds great,' said Sanchez. 'Perhaps Tim and I will be able to try it out. I've never ridden a thunderstorm.'

'How are we going to get these guests?' asked Big Mother. 'Should we advertise in the newspapers?'

Sigmond frowned slightly at this idea.

'Perhaps,' he said. 'But I myself have many contacts. There will be no difficulty in finding customers. When they hear of your boat they will come flocking.'

'Goodness!' said Sanchez. 'Aren't we lucky having a super antique starship to offer?'

'And all these super cups of cold unbrewed tea,' Tim added rather meanly.

'Ah!' Sigmond sighed. 'Ah!' There I see just one big difficulty.'

'You mean how are we going to feed paying guests who won't like my cooking?' Big Mother took his point.

'But do your humans like the same raw, uncooked cooking as elephants eat?' asked Tim.

'Of course they do,' said Sigmond. 'Once you have tried it everything else is like eating cinders.'

'Isn't this unheated food very easy to cook?' Sanchez suggested hopefully. 'Just salads and stuff?'

'Alas no,' Sigmond frowned. 'Our cooking is the most delicate in the galaxy. Our foods must be mixed and measured and weighed and pounded and steeped by the hour. Our list of herbs and spices is endless. When my sister and I hold a party at college we spend whole nights preparing in the kitchen. We are food artists.'

Morween tilted back her head and looked up at the ceiling. She whispered softly:

> *At the stove I cook my soul*
> *To give you soup in a silver bowl.*
> *Eat delicately tonight for with the food*
> *You eat my soul which I have stewed.*

Sanchez thought Morween was getting better with the rhymes, but Big Mother looked upset and there was an uneasy pause.

'My sister means that a good cook is giving you more than just a lettuce salad; she's giving you her personality,' Sigmond explained. 'I wish you could try some of her cooking.'

23

'Are the two of you actually working at your university just now?' Big Mother asked thoughtfully.

'Oh no!' Sigmond replied. 'Term only lasts a quarter of the year and the rest of our time is holiday.'

'Would you and your sister like to join us on the first of our cruises to act as cooks?' Big Mother suggested. 'We'd pay you well of course and you'd be doing us a real favour.'

'Then we could sample Morween's cooking,' Sanchez joined in.

'Sometimes, not every day,' said Tim hastily. 'I mean she'd be busy cooking for our guests most of the time, wouldn't she?'

Sigmond rolled his eyes at Tim as if he was sharing a joke.

'A holiday job would be admirable,' he said. 'Business and pleasure. But I always leave my sister to decide. She is twice the cook that I am.'

Everyone turned to look at Morween – who never seemed to look at anyone. She gazed out of the cabin windows at the rain, and said very softly:

> *'From far across the halls of space,*
> *Come humans of another race.*
> *What can we be to them but friends*
> *And join to serve each other's ends?'*

She smiled nervously.

'So that's settled,' said Sigmond briskly. 'My sister will cook and I'll be the waiter.'

'We haven't even sold the tracking equipment

yet,' Old Elias protested. He still hated the idea of towing a caravan through space.

'Leave everything to me,' said Sigmond, 'and all difficulties will vanish! I think I see a break in this light shower. We must get things moving. To the next time!'

The rain was pouring down harder than ever, but the elephants seemed able to see a light side to the heaviest downpour. As they climbed down out of the cabin they each activated a small force field strapped to their wrists and these kept the rain sliding down a watery egg shape with each elephant dry in the middle. As they got into the harness of their hang gliders Sigmond gave a farewell wave, and then, with a blast of the mini rockets on the wings, the two gliders soared up into the rain clouds and were gone.

'Well,' said Big Mother as she tipped their tea leaves and water into the disposer, 'that was luck, meeting such helpful elephants the minute we landed.'

'I wonder if it really was luck,' said Tim mysteriously. 'I mean, they've just about taken us over, haven't they?'

'Well, it was that or starve,' said Sanchez. 'I think it's sensible to be hopeful, just like Sigmond.'

'Meanwhile,' said Big Mother, 'I'll heat up the spaghetti.'

Chapter 2

Everything went just as Sigmond had said. Next day a gang of cheerful elephants came with a hover truck and carted all the electronic tracking gear off to an Auction Sale Room where it was sold for about half its real value. With the money Old Elias hired a luxury caravan trailer-glider and a tow rope a mile long. Then he flew *Dragonfall 5* over to Kantaroom Space Port and linked up with the caravan. By this time it was evening, so they all went out for a good meal at a restaurant as he had promised.

The food was elephant food and all unheated, but even Tim had to admit it was delicious.

'Like sinking into a hay field where you can eat all the flowers,' he said.

Next morning it had stopped raining and there was an advertisement in the main daily paper. It read:

ELEGANT VINTAGE CRUISE YACHT FOR HIRE

Dragonfall 5, a unique opportunity.
For a limited season this ancient
But perfectly maintained starship

Will cruise with select parties to
The Lost Home.
You will enjoy the ruined marvels of the dead
    cities
And the bracing experiences of Space.
You will relax while you sample our delicious
    cooking in
Your own private apartments
A mile
Away from engine noise and disturbance.
Terms by agreement at Kantaroom Space Port.

'It sounds like a poem,' said Tim. 'Did Morween
write it?'

'No,' said Big Mother, 'I did. Sigmond didn't
want me to, but I wasn't going to take chances on
people turning up. Though I say it myself, I think
it reads very well!'

'If I were rich and I'd seen that, I'd come rushing,'
Sanchez agreed.

'How much are we going to charge?' Tim asked.

'We'll suggest five hundred credits a day,' said Big
Mother, 'and drop to three hundred if they turn out
to be hard bargainers.'

'I suppose they'll be humans since we're cruising
to Lost Home,' said Sanchez sadly. 'Elephants are
much more fun.'

'Here's Sigmond now if you want fun,' said Tim.

A little hover scooter came bowling across the
Space Port. It had a brass canopy with bells at the
corners, and under the canopy were Sigmond and
his sister and a pile of luggage.

'Another bright morning!' Sigmond called out. 'I told you the rain was slacking off.'

'It went on for nearly two days after you said that,' Tim pointed out as they handed the luggage into the caravan.

'You gloomy humans! Where would you be without me?' Sigmond breezed about the caravan kitchen with pots and packages. He was wearing an indigo suede jumper suit with small bells on the pockets. Morween had on a long white dress in chamois leather, and a cluster of white plastic rings round her trunk.

'See!' Sigmond waved happily out across the Space Port. 'Your first guest is coming to arrange his luxury cruise.'

'Already!' Old Elias looked surprised. 'The paper has only just been delivered!'

'Ah, papers and advertisements!' Sigmond snorted scornfully. 'They are nothing. What you need are contacts!'

'Just look at that hover boat!' Sanchez exclaimed.

Whistling towards them over the tarmac at a steady seventy miles an hour was a most remarkable craft. The deck had begun by being white and gold, but someone had covered its sides with luminous paintings of humans eating and drinking and enjoying themselves. The cabin was made of carved green onyx inlaid with mother of pearl, and a long silken house flag streamed from the stern. As it approached *Dragonfall* it sounded a tremendous fanfare of recorded trumpets but did not stop. Instead it made a slow circle right round *Dragonfall* as if inspecting it, then settled with a sagging hiss a few yards away.

To the sound of a single trumpet a gangway extended to the ground and four heavily armed bodyguards, two elephants and two humans, trotted down. They took up positions covering all angles with their blasters and then a tall thin man in a long black cloak stalked down the gangway. He bowed to the watching crew of *Dragonfall* and stepped back to study the old starship with an admiring smile.

'What a prodigy!' he said.

Old Elias and Big Mother climbed down to meet the stranger and shake hands.

'Don't tell me these rocket pods are the original R.O. two-five-sixers!' were the tall man's first words.

'They certainly are,' said Old Elias. 'We could never afford replacements.'

'Not that we've ever needed them,' Big Mother added quickly. 'You can see the condition they're in.'

'Perfect!' The stranger ran a finger over the gleaming pods. 'And you still use them?'

'Every time we land or take off,' Old Elias confirmed.

'Marvellous! Now your galactic integrator, don't tell me you still use a model five?'

'None other!' said Old Elias firmly. 'On a 1500 tuning and it never puts a foot wrong.'

'In this day and age!' the tall man marvelled.

'Three weeks in hyperspace on our last journey,'

29

said Old Elias, 'and it never gave a moment's trouble.'

'What a beauty!' said the man. 'I suppose she's not for sale?'

'Never,' said Big Mother.

'How right,' said the man. 'It would be a crime to give up a ship like this. She's good for another hundred years. What are your hire charges?'

'Five hundred a day,' said Big Mother.

'Done!' said the man eagerly.

'A week's cash in advance,' Big Mother added bravely.

'Madam, we must go up into your cabin and sign the cheque now!'

Looking as if she got cheques for three thousand five hundred credits most mornings of the week, Big Mother climbed back up into *Dragonfall*. Tim, Sanchez and the two elephants had watched all this from the caravan kitchen.

'Wow!' said Sanchez. 'We've made a sale. We're safe again!'

'If he really is rich,' Tim put in doubtfully.

'Oh, that's Mr Algeveer,' said Sigmond. 'He's a multimillionaire. You don't have to worry about his cheques!'

'How does he make his money?' Sanchez asked.

'Well,' Sigmond looked vague and uneasy, 'this way and that, you know!'

'No, we don't know,' said Tim. 'That's why we asked.'

He looked Sigmond firmly in the eye.

'Oh, dealing; that sort of thing,' said Sigmond.

'And now if you'll excuse me I must change into my waiter's clothes. It wouldn't do to be caught wearing my student bells, would it?'

'Why not?' Tim wanted to know, but Sigmond had retreated into a cupboard and Morween was busy pounding herbs.

'We'd better go and meet Mr Algeveer,' said Tim. 'I'm sure I've heard his name before somewhere.'

'So have I,' Sanchez agreed. 'It was in the newspapers a few months back, but I can't remember what it was all about.'

In the cabin Mr Algeveer had signed the cheque and was sitting at the controls, having them explained to him by Old Elias.

'What an experience!' he said. 'And you are the lucky lads who drive this wonderful old ship all over the universe. It's a privilege to meet you. You don't know how fortunate you are. Ah me!'

Suddenly Mr Algeveer looked very unhappy. He sighed again.

'Ah me! What a wasted life I have had! What opportunities I have missed!'

Dragonfall's crew gazed at him as he sat slumped in the control seat.

'If you like,' Old Elias suggested helpfully, 'you can take over the controls yourself when we're out in space.'

'How kind, how very kind!' But Mr Algeveer still looked gloomy. He shook his head and got up.

'And now you must meet my family and we will inspect our living quarters.'

They climbed down again and Mr Algeveer waved

31

commandingly to the cabin of the great hover boat. Two women dressed in grey and a short plump man in another black cloak came down the gangway to meet them.

'I want you to meet my lady wife,' Mr Algeveer beckoned to the first of the two women, 'and Aunt Melinda and the Uncle.'

Aunt Melinda was a thin, frail woman with a bright nervous smile; she had the trick of snapping her fingers like soft castanets. The Uncle Algeveer, her husband, looked much more jolly, though he kept his eyes carefully on his brother to see when he should be laughing and when he should be serious.

Everyone shook hands and said how pleasant the weather was.

'It is decided, my dear,' Mr Algeveer addressed his wife. 'The ship is perfect. We shall all holiday in her for the next few weeks. We shall ride the thunderstorms of the Antonin Mountains and perhaps see a few plays in the Intergalactic Theatre Festival at the Old City. Exercise for the body and food for the brain, you will enjoy that, eh!'

'How nice!' said Mrs Algeveer. She was a subdued, anxious, little woman. 'And perhaps a few quiet days in some remote health farm. My husband, you know,' she turned to Big Mother, 'has had a very disturbed time lately and needs rest and quiet, rest and quiet.'

Mr Algeveer snorted and looked uneasily towards his four bodyguards with their blasters.

'Quite true, my dear,' he agreed. 'We need to get

away from here for a while into a different atmosphere. But where is my daughter? She must meet her new young friends. Where is Karanda?'

'Here, father,' a girl put her head out of a window in the hover boat and looked severely down at them. 'I am waiting for my trumpet!'

Mr Algeveer signed hastily up to the control of the hover boat. A silvery trumpet played a long flourish and the girl, dressed in prim black and white stripes, appeared at the top of the gangway. When the trumpet finished she walked down the steps holding herself very straight.

'This is Karanda,' said Mr Algeveer proudly and managing a little smile again. 'She is our daughter and our only child.'

Karanda shook hands with the whole of *Dragonfall*'s crew; her hand was very cool. She scratched Jerk behind his left ear but never once smiled.

'We are going thunder riding in the Antonins, my dear,' her mother told her. 'You'll enjoy that, won't you?'

'Thunderstorms will be peaceful after what we've been putting up with lately,' said Karanda in a sad little voice. 'They won't come after us there, will they?'

Mr Algeveer looked warily in the direction of the space port buildings.

'If we get away from Pine Home for a few days they'll forget about us and turn their attentions to someone else,' he said.

'Are you in some sort of trouble here?' Big Mother asked. 'Can we help?'

'Nothing, nothing to matter,' said Mr Algeveer quickly. 'Nothing that a few weeks' holiday won't put right. Why, when I ...'

'Golly,' Sanchez interrupted rudely, 'There's an absolute fleet of hang gliders coming up on the east wind.' He pointed behind *Dragonfall*, away from the space port. 'There must be hundreds of them!'

And there were; a whole armada of coloured sails was coasting in silently on the strong east wind, flying at anything from near ground level to five hundred feet. Several of the hang gliders were linked together with large banners that had writing on them in elephant language, all squiggles and blots.

'Not again!' Mr Algeveer wailed.

'We will never escape them,' cried Mrs Algeveer.

'Oh my! oh my!' said the Aunt, 'when do they get any sleep? They were at it all last night!' She snapped her fingers in agitation.

Only Karanda was icy calm.

'Bodyguard!' she called in a stony voice. 'Blasters set for whirlwind discharge and scatter this rabble! No tear gas because the wind is blowing our way.'

The four bodyguards saluted, adjusted their blaster charges and knelt to fire the heavy weapons. A chorus of shouts and slogans in elephant language was drifting down the wind to *Dragonfall* from the glider armada.

'Minims, come quickly!' Sanchez called up to the

cabin. As the little animals came scurrying eagerly down to his shoulder the four blasters erupted into an ear-shattering shriek of sound.

'Look at that!' Tim gasped.

Four jets of wind were sweeping the hang gliders from the sky as the blasters raked them. Some tilted sideways and slipped, some sails ballooned and swirled up on artificial thermals of air, others fluttered earthwards in circles, sprouting parachutes as their flyers escaped. Most of the gliders, however, took refuge in their rocket boosters and shot a mile away to safety on dense columns of white smoke.

For one minute the noise was appalling. Sanchez saw Karanda's mouth move in an order. The next second the four blasters were still and the silence was like fresh air.

Karanda had not budged from where she first stood. The bodyguard watched her respectfully for the next order.

'Now, father,' she turned to Mr Algeveer who was wringing his hands nervously, 'in five minutes this rabble will have reformed and returned to the attack.'

'And this evening,' Mr Algeveer said gloomily, 'we will be facing police charges for using too much force.'

Karanda smiled contemptuously and nodded towards the space port.

'Another group is approaching on foot and will be harder to scatter.'

She was right. A crowd of elephants was marching

towards them in broad formation, chanting as they came. They sounded rather threatening.

'I think we ought to leave.' Mr Algeveer turned to Old Elias.

'For where?' Old Elias hastily crammed his still burning pipe into his pocket.

'For Lost Home and the Antovin Mountains,' Karanda rapped out.

'But when?' Old Elias turned from the fluttering hang gliders as they reformed, to the distant crowd as it chanted.

'Start your engines now,' Karanda ordered. 'We leave in two minutes! Mother, the luggage!'

Mr Algeveer nodded hastily to Old Elias. Karanda stood firing orders at her family, the body-guards and the crew of the hover boat. Everyone sprang into action. The black-clad Algeveers ran like a speeded-up film back to the cabin of the hover boat, then out to the caravan glider which was lying tilted behind *Dragonfall*. The crew of the hover boat rushed after them dragging folded hang gliders and bales of luggage along the ground, and Sigmond popped up to help. He looked quite different in the black and white leathers of his waiter's clothes. Elephants have a huge advantage when it comes to carrying things because they can use their trunks as a third hand. The work went fast.

Karanda stood watching the second hand of her watch.

'Fifty seconds ... One minute ... Right!' she called.

All the luggage had been hurled pell mell into the

caravan. The Algeveers were all aboard except Karanda.

'Ready?' she snapped up at Old Elias as he sat at the controls.

'Rockets away, Admiral!' Old Elias nodded back. Sanchez, who had been standing in the open door to let the Minims hear the chanting, jumped inside and slammed the door. The elephants marching from the space port broke into a run, waving their banners and posters wildly. A few squashy fruits which they were throwing landed on the bright decks of the hover boat.

Karanda turned and motioned the hover boat to move off. Its engines began to hiss, the crowd roared.

'Captain!' Karanda had turned back and was looking up at *Dragonfall*. She was a small black and white figure in the centre of all the hurry and din.

'Yes?' Old Elias flipped back a port window to hear her.

'You did not put out your pipe. As a result your trousers are on fire. Pilots must keep cool!'

Just for a second Karanda gave a little smile, then skipped lightly over to where her father waited at the door of the caravan.

'She's right!' Big Mother said, and dashed a saucepan of water over the back of Old Elias's trousers. 'That girl has a calm head.'

'Rockets to force eight!' Old Elias ordered, patting his pants.

'Force eight!' Tim repeated at the controls.

Their rocket pods fired twin pillars of golden flame. Next to them the hover boat had risen whistling on its skirts and was wobbling away to the left to escape the anger of the crowd.

'Power on the port rocket,' Old Elias ordered. 'Swing her to starboard well away from that box of hot air. We'll go the other way over the hang gliders.'

'We'll have to climb like mad!' Tim protested.

'Nothing this bird can't do in an emergency,' Old Elias declared. 'Gun her engines and she'll reply!'

'Remember the caravan,' Big Mother warned. She had sat down and begun her knitting – a sure danger sign.

'No back-seat driving,' Old Elias snarled.

With her left-hand rocket pod spouting a fountain of fire *Dragonfall* swung round in a circle. Tim raised her up a few feet on her anti-gravs in the nick of time to avoid tangling with the tow rope as they cut back across it.

'Now! Full power,' roared Old Elias.

Both pods coughed flames that turned from gold to white hot. The tarmac melted and fumed. *Dragonfall 5* quivered from end to end, then rose on her tail and literally hurled herself, like a blue and silver bolt, towards the cloudy heavens.

'I wonder how the caravan will take it?' Sanchez jumped up on to his bunk to look back from the bulge of the cabin roof. *Dragonfall* was gaining speed, going up almost straight. The mile of tow line was looping up after them, but the caravan glider with its stubby streamlined fins still lay undisturbed on the ground.

'She'll look after herself,' said Old Elias confidently. 'She's designed for that. She's gyro-stabilised on automatic anti-gravity units.'

'Do you think Sigmond's remembered to switch them on?' Tim asked.

'If he hasn't, Karanda will,' said Sanchez. 'Karanda remembers everything!'

'Angle our climb off to forty-five degrees,' Old Elias ordered. 'That'll make take-off easier for them. We're well above those pesky hang-glider critters now.'

Dragonfall eased her climb a little. At that instant Sanchez saw the caravan take the tow. It twitched into line and shot up after them, climbing easily on a level keel as its stabilisers corrected its flight.

'There won't be a plate spilt in the dining-room or a cup in the kitchen,' Old Elias declared in satisfaction. 'Luxury cruise was what we said and luxury cruise is what we'll give them.'

Towing a mile below *Dragonfall*, the caravan swooped through the cloud of hang gliders, sending them jetting away again in all directions.

'I bet they'll get a tomato or two on their windows,' said Sanchez.

'If Karanda hasn't trained her blasters on them,' Tim laughed.

Dragonfall, still on top rocket power, was climbing out of the thinning atmosphere of Pine Home at twenty-seven thousand miles an hour. Already they could see the curve of the planet and the green patterns of its forests through their rear window. Ahead of them Lost Home glowed like a tawny eye

41

in the dark heavens. Soon they would be able to swing their galactic integrator, the model five that Mr Algeveer had admired, into star drive. Then they would be moving faster than light through hyperspace and, provided Old Elias had worked his sums out right, they would pop out again seconds later into real space only a few thousand miles from Lost Home. Of course it would be a very different story if Old Elias had got his figures wrong. Sometimes when that happened they ended up further away than they had started.

Tim switched on the automatic pilot and turned to face the rest of the family.

'Just what do we think is going on with these Algeveers?' he demanded. 'Ten minutes after he's hired us we're in the middle of a crash take-off to escape, not just one, but two crowds of demonstrators.'

'Poor fellow,' said Old Elias. 'He's being hounded! That's what's happening.'

'That Aunt said that the demonstrators had been after them all the previous night,' Sanchez added. 'I heard her.'

'And Karanda was obviously used to dealing with them,' said Tim admiringly.

'I think she was unnecessarily rough,' said Big Mother firmly. 'Someone might have got hurt. We don't want to get involved with the police.'

'How do you think Mr Algeveer made all his money?' asked Tim.

'Sigmond said "by dealing",' Sanchez reminded them. 'But he didn't really want to tell us, did he?'

'No,' said Tim eagerly. 'And there's another odd

thing. I think it was Sigmond who brought Mr Algeveer hurrying along to hire us, not that advert in the newspaper.'

'Yet Sigmond didn't seem to know him,' said Sanchez. 'Do you remember how keen he was to get into his waiter's uniform.'

'Yes,' Tim puzzled, 'and why?'

'So that he wouldn't look like a student!' Sanchez suggested.

'I don't blame him. Those pesky students are always rushing around in crowds with banners demonstrating against people,' Old Elias joined in.

'But Sigmond has been a student for fourteen years,' said Sanchez. 'He must be a superstudent by now!'

'Do you mean,' Big Mother asked seriously, 'that we're just part of a plot organised by a couple of student elephants?'

'It looks very much like that,' said Tim. 'Remember how they were waiting for us in that factory yard? I believe Sigmond arranged for Mr Algeveer to be told about *Dragonfall* yesterday, then fixed to have demonstrators bother him all last night. That made the poor man come hurrying down here this morning to escape. It's a put-up job and that's why Sigmond doesn't want to look like a student. But he's the mastermind in the middle of it all!'

'Careful!' warned Sanchez. 'If it weren't for Sigmond we'd still be eating spaghetti in that factory yard. Instead we've got money in our pockets and we're off on a holiday cruise.'

'To ride thunderstorms on a bit of canvas!' Old Elias sniffed.

'Minims!' Sanchez called.

They popped their heads out of his pockets where they had been waiting their turn.

'What did it say on all those banners?' Sanchez asked.

The Minims looked at each other doubtfully.

'They were descriptions of Mr Algeveer,' said the first.

'But not necessarily accurate,' said the second.

'Never mind. Tell us a few,' Tim suggested. Minims often had to be coaxed because they hated translating untruths and they heard so many.

'One notice described him as a merchant of death,' said the first.

'Another as a shark with a wide open mouth,' said the second.

'A third urged him to go away and eat worms,' said the last.

'That's not very helpful, is it?' asked Sanchez.

'We said it was not necessarily accurate,' the first Minim reminded him.

'What was the crowd chanting?' Tim asked.

'A poem,' replied the second Minim promptly.

'A very bad one,' added the third.

'Never mind,' Sanchez persuaded. 'We won't blame you. Tell it to us.'

The Minims put their heads together for a second or two, then chanted in deep voices together, sounding just like a crowd though there were only the three of them:

> '*Al – ge – veer*
> *Is a name of fear.*
> *You don't want him there*
> *And we don't want him here.*'

'A name of fear,' Tim repeated thoughtfully, 'and a merchant of death. Those seem to go together.'

'And he does wear black,' Sanchez added.

'This is getting worrying,' said Big Mother. She looked back to where the caravan rode a mile behind them, brilliant with lights but lonely and tiny compared with the great green orb of Pine Home and the white brilliance of Khosro Khai, the mega-strength star.

'Nonsense,' Old Elias snorted, Mr Algeveer is a born engineer, sound as they come. He knows a real starship when he sees one. He'll look after himself.'

'But,' Tim insisted, 'it does look as if a lot of elephants dislike him and Sigmond does seem to have managed it so that he and Morween are alone with the Algeveers . . .'

'Cooking for them!' Sanchez interrupted. 'What about poison?'

'That settles it!'

Big Mother seized the telephone that linked them with the caravan and rang through.

There was a long long pause while the bell rang and the family waited tensely.

'Perhaps they're lying stiff and cold!' said Sanchez gloomily.

His mother frowned, but at that moment the phone was picked up at the other end.

'Yes?' Mr Algeveer's voice sounded irritable but healthy.

'*Dragonfall* reporting to caravan,' said Big Mother, 'to wish you a good night's sleep and to ask if everything is to your satisfaction.'

'Much better than that, everything is perfect!' Mr Algeveer replied decisively. 'After a feast of delicious food your cook is now favouring us with a feast of wonderful poetry. What a treasure! Excuse me but I must go. She is still reciting. I must not miss a word. We will talk when we reach the Antovin Mountains at sunrise tomorrow. Good night.'

The phone clicked off and the *Dragonfall* family sat feeling rather foolish.

'So much for your student plots and master minds,' said Big Mother. 'Morween is entertaining them with poetry.'

'Oh!' said Tim lamely. 'But it did look odd, didn't it? We had to be sure.'

'Perhaps,' said Big Mother. 'But there's enough trouble and suspicion around without our adding to it. The best thing we can do now is get a good night's rest. Tomorrow it will be our turn to keep the Algeveers happy.'

Chapter 3

'They're coming in again to dive bomb!' Sanchez called.

He was lying on his back in his hammock. High up against a blue-black sky the five hang gliders were gathering in a fan shape for an attack on the starship.

'Not again!' Tim groaned at the controls as he kept *Dragonfall* idling on her anti-gravs. 'What'll they throw this time?'

Big Mother looked up from her cooking.

'It was flour last time. Now they've only got to squirt water and there'll be pancakes plastered all over my clean fuselage!'

'They're swooping,' Sanchez reported.

The Algeveers' black and white hang gliders were nosing sharply down in tight formation. From time to time Sanchez could see flecks of light as the safety wires that linked the gliders to *Dragonfall* caught the glare of the great sun. Out here, off Lost Home, Khosro Khai burned in the heavens eight times larger than the sun of Earth. Nothing escaped its harsh light.

'Strafed by a load of amateurs!' Tim said crossly.

'And not able to fire back,' Sanchez complained. 'What a job!'

It was the first full day of the luxury cruise and of keeping the Algeveers happy. *Dragonfall* was moored twenty thousand feet above the Antovin Mountains of Lost Home and her crew was earning five hundred credits a day the hard way. They were finding out what Sigmond had meant when he told them that the humans of Pine Home had a peculiar sense of humour.

The trouble had begun when they arrived at sunrise over the Antovins and found that there were no thunderstorms. Mr Algeveer had been very put out. He had promised Karanda that she should have thunderstorms to ride in her hang glider and instead there was clear calm air. So he had come jetting out from the caravan in his hang glider to discuss what they should do.

Old Elias had been splendid with him. First he had let him pilot *Dragonfall* through a few exciting turns and manoeuvres. Then, when Mr Algeveer was beaming with pleasure, Old Elias had suggested war games until the next thunderstorm rolled up.

'Dummy runs, mock ammunition!' Mr Algeveer exclaimed. 'Karanda will love it. How kind!'

Nothing would satisfy him in his morning high spirits but that Old Elias should accept one of his cigars. Then, he insisted on lighting it for him, though Old Elias would much rather have cut it up and smoked it in his pipe. A few minutes later, as Mr Algeveer was making a great show of preparing to leave, the cigar blew up with a loud report and the front two inches of it turned into a firework which orbited around the cabin with a shrill whining

48

noise. Mr Algeveer roared with delighted laughter at this and Old Elias, after putting out the sparks in his beard, managed a brave smile.

When Mr Algeveer had flown back to prepare for his war game the *Dragonfall* family looked at each other.

'Oh dear,' said Sanchez. 'They like practical jokes!'

'That's what Sigmond meant about his humans,' said Tim. 'They go up and down; sometimes they're high-spirited and sometimes they're depressed. No wonder the elephants feel superior.'

'It must be the result of losing their own world all those years ago,' Big Mother put in reasonably. 'That must be very gloom-making.'

49

Old Elias came back from washing the soot off his face.

'If we got to work and split that tow rope,' he said, 'we could make it two miles long instead of one. I'd like that!'

But Big Mother had reminded them of the money shortage, so all the day they had patiently acted as target while the whole Algeveer family played at being dive bombers. This was their tenth run. Tim was allowed to wobble *Dragonfall* on her anti-gravs but not to move her with rocket power when the Algeveers glided in with their flour bags.

'I've lost sight of one,' Sanchez reported.

'That'll be the Aunt,' said Tim. 'She's always messing up her turns. Here come the others!'

As the four gliders swooped down Tim rolled *Dragonfall* towards them on an air current, presenting a perfect target. The leading Algeveer glider hesitated in flight, suspicious that things were too easy, expecting a lurch away as the flour bags were released. Tim at the controls began just such a tiny movement, the hang gliders swerved to counter it then, at the second the flour bombs flew, Tim swung *Dragonfall* back on to its earlier roll, escaping three of the bombs and catching only one of them.

Fthud!

'Got me!' Sanchez moaned and pretended to flop wounded in his hammock.

'Missed the cabin completely,' Old Elias called triumphantly. 'There'll be no windows to clean.'

Then, straight out of the sun's glare, the fifth hang glider swept down upon them.

'This is curtains, folks!' Karanda's cheerful voice came from the inter-com radio.

Fthud!

'Oh no!' said Big Mother.

Karanda's flour bomb burst squarely on the zircon glass roof within inches of Sanchez's face. Flour spread all over the visi-dome, cutting visibility to nothing; the cabin went as dark as if a light switch had been turned off.

More cheerful voices and snuffly laughter came through the radio.

'Bull's-eye!'

'There's my little girl!'

'Drop your guns and reach for the sky!'

'Do you surrender?'

Dragonfall's crew sat in cross silence. Mr Algeveer's voice cut through the others.

'How was that, Captain? A fair cop, eh? Karanda is a born battle pilot. Shall we call it a day now and go home for some dinner?'

Old Elias gritted his teeth

'Whatever you say, Mr Algeveer. Yes, that was great shooting.'

'Home then,' Mr Algeveer continued, 'and we'll beg a tow lift back from you because the wind is blowing straight in our teeth.'

Tim tuned up a vibrator pitch and shook the worst of the flour off. The five hang gliders were lined up alongside *Dragonfall*'s cabin with the Algeveers waving and laughing happily. Suddenly Mr Algeveer gave a signal and the whole family reached down to pull gleaming black blasters out of flying suit harnesses. The grills of five sinister muzzles pointed threateningly at *Dragonfall*.

'Hey, watch out!' gasped Sanchez.

'Dad drat it! They'll go too far! I knew it,' Old Elias rasped.

The Algeveers fired together.

A puff of smoke and a large piece of paper came from each gun. As the smoke cleared the pieces of paper hung from the guns. They read:

BANG   BANG   BANG   BANG   BANG

More whoops of laughter came through the inter-com radio.

'Reach for the skies!'

'Your dinner or your lives!'

'Bang! Bang! You get it?'

Old Elias looked very grim.

'Towing these gliders back to the caravan is going to be a delicate operation,' he said. 'I'll just handle the controls for a few minutes.'

He took over Tim's seat and eased the old ship gently out of the full anti-gravity on which she had been riding the air currents. With a feathery touch of power from the right wing rocket he swung the ship in a careful left turn. The Algeveer family steered their gliders into a tight V formation behind the star drive in *Dragonfall*'s tail unit, and rode there comfortably, waiting for their tow. Inside the cabin everyone watched Old Elias uneasily.

'Prepare to take the strain,' he spoke into the inter-com.

'Gideeup, old mare!' Mr Algeveer called back and laughed jollily.

Old Elias switched off the radio.

'Seems to me,' he growled, 'that my rocket pods need decoking.'

He stabbed at the controls. The rockets began to thunder. He stabbed again and Tim saw that he had turned Thrust to its Off position. Though the rumble of the rocket motors rose even louder there were no flames coming from the pods.

'Dad,' Tim protested, 'you've got power at full strength but no combustion.'

'Have I now!' Old Elias didn't sound a bit worried as he looked back at the black and white sails ranged just above and behind *Dragonfall*. 'I'll give them a count of five to let the pressure build up, then give them a real clean out!

'Five –

'Four –

'Three –

'Two –'

'You'll smother them in soot!' Big Mother warned.

'One –

'Zero!'

Old Elias switched Thrust back to On position. For a moment *Dragonfall* seemed to hiccup. Then each rocket pod coughed a cloud of oily soot backwards and flamed into life. The old starship lurched forward. Behind her, streaming in the exhaust wave, rode five bleared and smoky hang gliders piloted by five coal-black Algeveers.

'Golly!' said Sanchez.

'What have you done?' exclaimed Big Mother.

'Shown them we've got a sense of humour,' said Old Elias. 'They enjoy a laugh.'

For a few moments the radio was sinisterly quiet. Then a steely ripple came from the speaker.

It was Karanda laughing.

Next Mr Algeveer joined in with his snuffly laughter and soon all five Algeveers were giggling and chortling away on their sooty gliders.

'Seems I've got a speck of dust in my eye,' Karanda reported. 'Now how about you *Dragonfallers* having dinner with us this evening to talk it all over and let Morween show you what real Pine Home cooking is like? Will you come over?'

Old Elias shook his head furiously at Big Mother. He could imagine rubber spiders in his salad and chairs being pulled away when he sat down. Big Mother took the microphone.

'We wish we could, Karanda,' she said, 'but with these tricky air currents and a big thunderhead showing up on the weather predictor Old Elias and I will have to stay aboard. But the boys will be pleased to visit you. Thank you very much.'

Tim looked at Sanchez and Sanchez looked at Tim. Both shook their heads.

'Parents!' said Sanchez.

After the Algeveers had been towed back they needed an hour to have good hot baths. Then *Dragonfall* pulled alongside the caravan's entrance port and the two boys stepped carefully through the air lock. They took Jerk with them.

'Welcome aboard,' Karanda smiled. 'I was look-ing forward to a chat, and I hear there will be a big thunderstorm soon. We'll have a grand time!'

'Oh yes,' said Sanchez. He was nervous of thun-derstorms and of Karanda.

They shook hands again with all the Algeveers then, while Tim tried to find out about the student demonstrations, Sanchez slipped off to see how Sig-mond and Morween were getting on in the kitchen. Morween was cooking and singing in elephant lan-guage. As usual she seemed more interested in the ceiling than in anything else, but Sigmond was in fine form.

'Wonderful trip,' he told Sanchez. 'Everyone loves us – my music, Morween's poetry, my waiting, Morween's cooking, your starship and now this war game. You should have seen them when they got back! Black from head to foot! You did a good job there, but watch out for Karanda.'

'Why?' asked Sanchez.

'She's a very self-willed girl. She's out to give you a rough ride on this next thunderstorm.'

'What am I going to do?'

'Ride it out. Don't worry, you'll be quite safe in a force field even if it does get bumpy. I'll see you're all right.'

'I suppose you know the Algeveers quite well?' Sanchez asked casually.

'Know them!' Sigmond looked wary. 'Never met them until last night.'

'Oh, we thought you must have told them about us.'

'Let's say I know someone who knows someone else who knows the Algeveers,' Sigmond said carefully. 'So word about *Dragonfall* might have got passed around. I warned you about their sense of humour, but otherwise they're splendid people and very rich.'

'How did you say they made their money?' Sanchez tried again. 'That crowd of elephants at the space port were calling them "merchants of death". They didn't seem to think they were splendid at all.'

A tricky light shone in Sigmond's eye.

'I suppose they could say that,' he replied thoughtfully. 'It all depends on your point of view. Elephants do have to watch humans quite carefully. Humans work hard, but sometimes at the wrong things.'

'Like what?' Sanchez felt he was getting near the truth.

'Like making arms and armaments and selling them all over the galaxy,' Sigmond said quietly. 'Not that I've anything against it, of course. The Algeveers are very nice people and someone's got to do it.'

'They make guns and blasters, do they? I thought I knew the name,' said Sanchez. 'It's been worrying me.'

'It's been worrying a few people,' Sigmond replied, 'as you saw at the space port. Have you ever heard of the A.U. Destructor?'

'Yes. It's a weapon that can separate a whole planet from its sun, isn't it?' Sanchez remembered.

'And send it swinging out into darkness,' said Sigmond seriously. 'It's the ultimate weapon. Nothing could be more terrible.'

'What does A.U. stand for?' Sanchez asked, feeling sure he knew the answer.

'Algeveer's Universal!' Sigmond picked up a glass and began to polish it. 'Algeveer's Universal Destructor!'

'And Mr Algeveer invented it himself?' Sanchez continued.

'My father was the chairman of a company that put some money into developing the A.U. Destructor,' said a cool voice from the kitchen door.

It was Karanda and she was looking very firm. Sigmond went on polishing glasses furiously. Morween dropped a sieve and stopped singing.

'But you will understand that my father is on a rest holiday,' Karanda went on. 'We don't like to have him bothered with idle gossip about his work. He puts all that behind him.'

Sigmond snatched up a bowl of fruit salad in each hand and a jug of dressing with his trunk.

'Dinner is served,' he said, and turned out of the door.

'Father only makes arms for people to be able to defend themselves,' Karanda told Sanchez. 'He never sells them to people who will use them to attack other people.'

'Oh, good!' said Sanchez soothingly. 'Then that's all right.'

'Elephants don't understand,' Karanda finished sadly. 'They think you can play around all day and enjoy yourself, and because we don't do that
57

they chase after us with banners and shout horrid things.'

Morween picked up a bowl of herbs and turned to look at Karanda. Then she began to recite gently.

'If you can't love your fellows
Then leave them alone
Till the old quarrel mellows
And a new friend has grown.
For the whole of our galaxy, here is one law:
There never is a cause worth killing people for.'

Just for a moment Karanda looked as if she were going to burst into tears, but then her eyes hardened. 'We go to dinner,' she said.

Chapter 4

Dinner was served in the back room of the caravan where a broad balcony opened out on to a twenty-thousand-foot drop to the wrinkled surface of the Antovin Mountains. Though the food was delicious it was an uneasy meal. When Sanchez first sat down his cushion carried him up on miniature anti-gravs and suspended him over the table. The Algeveers loved that and laughed and clapped, but it wasn't the kind of event that helped you to relax. All through the meal the rumble of the approaching thunderstorm grew louder and the air was tense and still.

Dragonfall 5 and her caravan had drifted into a valley of cloud between two great banks of cumulonimbus that cut off the sinking sun. Before the second course, which was a great heap of sliced greengages and powdered pecan nuts, Sigmond came around lighting long blue candles because it had grown so dark. The black walls of cloud were alive with little bursts of lightning and it was plain that a dreadful storm was brewing.

'Our home planet welcomes us with thunder,' Mr Algeveer waved his hand towards the storm clouds.

'You still think of this as your home, do you?' Tim asked politely.

'Always,' said Mr Algeveer.

'Why not tell them the story of Lost Home and Chutar's Ride? Then they will understand how you feel,' Sigmond suggested in a very smooth voice from the sideboard, where he was piling up dishes.

'An excellent idea.' Mr Algeveer nibbled at a banana steeped in bay leaves and orange water, then began.

'Long ago, almost a thousand years, all our people lived here upon this desert planet. Though we built gliders to soar from the mountains we had no space travel. Pine Home was unvisited – just a light in our evening skies. But each year the rains were less, the rivers shrank and the deserts grew. Finally it was clear to us that, if we could not conquer space and cross to the other planet, most of our people would die of thirst and starvation.

'So a great prize was offered and for fifty years our inventors designed and our engineers con-structed. We built bigger gliders, airships, then aero-planes, but none of them was powerful enough to escape from our dying planet. We tried the electrical transmission of matter, but that was no good. Who wanted to come out at the other end transmitted into mixed-up pieces!'

Mr Algeveer looked sad as he remembered all the mixed-up pieces.

'You tried rockets in the end, I expect,' Tim helped him.

'Many times and failed,' Mr Algeveer replied.

'Our heroes died, consumed with their own fire. My people said that the Spirits of the Air were angry and punished us. Finally a great hero called Chutar built a rocket on a new principle. He took off in this new rocket ship and never came back.'

'What happened? Did he reach Pine Home?' asked Tim.

'No one knows. It is thought that he rose many hundreds of miles into the stratosphere and became trapped in orbit, doomed forever to circle the planet he loved, alone for all eternity.'

'Goodness!' said Sanchez, looking round at the Algeveers' gloomy faces, 'so that was another setback?'

'Not at all,' Mr Algeveer explained. 'Chutar had proved that this new rocket drive was powerful enough to escape our gravity. All our scientists set to work to harness what we called Chutar's Drive. Within four years a rocket ship had crossed to Pine Home and returned to tell of rivers, brimming seas and friendly elephants.'

Sigmond in his waiter's uniform bowed and Mr Algeveer nodded to him.

'Hearing of this welcome our people built a hundred rocket ships and soon they were streaming across space. Each year there were more humans on the new moist planet, fewer and fewer on the old dry one. Until, in the end, we called it not Home, but Lost Home.

'So now no one lives there?' asked Sanchez.

'A few hundred humans remain to look after the old buildings and care for the tourists,' replied Mr

Algeveer. 'Also a number of elephants live there who suffer from colds and enjoy the dry climate. You will realise that to an elephant a cold in the nose is a serious illness. In Lost Home they find relief. But all we humans love it still and travel back from time to time to visit the old glories of our race, though since Chutar's time the heavens are open to us.'

'That's really interesting,' said Tim. 'Fancy having to invent a space ship or die!'

'But no one ever found Chutar to bury him?' Sanchez asked. 'It must have been horrid to die all alone up there.'

Mr Algeveer shivered. Lightning and candlelight played on his face.

'Some people say he still rides,' he continued in a very low voice. 'At times of disaster his great rocket ship is seen flaming through the skies with Chutar standing dead at the controls!'

'A ghost rocket!' Sanchez was fascinated. 'Like the Flying Dutchman.'

'To see it is very bad luck.' Mr Algeveer shook his head; the rest of his family, even Karanda, looked frightened.

'You don't believe all this, do you?' Tim asked.

'Well,' began Mr Algeveer uncertainly.

He never got any further. A tremendous flash of lightning lit the cabin and the walls of the cloud valley.

Crash! The door flew open. Smash! went the pile of glasses Sigmond was carrying as, with a miserable whimper, Jerk half flew, half jumped, through the door, over the table and on to Sanchez's lap, knocking him right off his low chair.

'One . . . two . . .' Tim counted.

A concussive roar of thunder shook the skies, seeming to rattle right inside their heads.

'At last!' Karanda jumped up from the table beaming with pleasure. 'Now we can stormride!'

She skipped out on to the balcony and began unfolding her black hang glider. The rest followed her.

To Sanchez the view from the balcony was worrying. Several miles below them were the peaks of desolate hills. On each side of them dark vapour boiled and swirled with the pressures of the storm. Even within its secure force field the caravan dipped and swayed as the two thunderheads collided about them. But Karanda, her father and her uncle were busy preparing for their favourite sport. Karanda fixed her glider wing open, activated the frail wiring of the force field, then secured her safety line to the balcony rail, and she was ready.

'You will enjoy this,' she told Sanchez. 'Hurry, you can use my aunt's glider and Tim can borrow my mother's. Father will lead us off.'

Mr Algeveer, strapped into his glider, was sitting poised on the rail of the balcony. With a smart kick of his legs he was away, out into the void, rising unexpectedly above and behind them like a large kite.

'What about the lightning?' Sanchez asked. 'Won't it strike him?'

'They must have perfected a small force field,' Tim explained. 'Everyone says they're wizards at electronics. But I should have thought . . .'

'Look!' gasped Sanchez.

A lightning flash crackled down on to the little glider and its pilot, balling around them in an explosion of light.

'He's had it!' Sanchez whispered.

'No, he hasn't!' Tim shouted in excitement. 'See, he's up there. Inside the force field he just bounces like a rubber ball.'

Mr Algeveer was hanging where the force of the lightning had hurled his craft a clear hundred feet higher. He was waving and obviously back in high spirits again.

'Last one to leave is a chicken,' Karanda spoke mockingly from her bat wing. Uncle Algeveer kicked off from the rail to join his brother as the lightning struck again. The gliders flew left and right like toys.

'In theory nothing can go wrong.' Tim fastened himself carefully into his harness and fixed his safety line. 'And if it does, we are all linked up by these headphones so we can contact each other.' He waited for a gap in the lightning, then jumped awkwardly from a standing position on the rail. An eddy of wind swirled him up and out of sight.

Sanchez clipped himself hurriedly into the awkward spread of sail. His shoulders felt half a mile wide, but he was determined not to be last. It was no good thinking what might go wrong. Modern science had made these gliders foolproof. No one got killed any longer. He scrambled on to the balcony rail.

64

'Hey!' Karanda shouted. 'Do you usually jump like that?'

'Yes. Why not?' Sanchez asked firmly.

'Because you haven't fastened your safety line! You'd never have got back.'

He watched her fasten his line securely to a pressure clip; kept his mind a blank; then jumped.

For a minute he rode there at the full stretch of the safety line. The caravan looked tiny. Wind and rain lashed his forehead, but the wonderful thing was that he was part of the wind. It didn't frighten him, he went with it. Then . . . Scramble! Pam! Kerpow! Splatt! and all the other 'wham' words. The lightning seized him in a white flame and instantly he was somewhere else. Mr Algeveer was to his right; somehow the caravan had got above him and quite close.

Again and again the lightning struck. Now Sanchez understood the chortling and singing in his earphones from the other gliders. To be bounced about by lightning and ride the wind itself was the greatest sport of all. He wanted the storm to rage for ever.

After twenty minutes there came a lull as the storm circled. The cloud valley still held its shape and some lightning still rippled in the walls of vapour, but no flashes stabbed them where the five hang gliders rode in the clear central space.

Then it happened.

Out of the blackness where the planet's wild hills were hidden in night a great white rocket was rising slowly, deliberately, on a pillar of red fire. No one saw its launching flare. One minute there was darkness, the next there was the rocket. It mounted up almost exactly midway between *Dragonfall 5* and her tow. From their hang gliders the five had a grandstand seat.

Mr Algeveer saw it, shut his eyes quickly and moaned with terror.

Tim saw it and counted eight clumsy rockets fastened to its iron sides with makeshift rods and bolts. He was surprised that it was so old-fashioned, but it was belching plenty of fire.

Sanchez saw the crest on the side: a black sword brandished by a black arm, and noted the lonely pinpoint of light which must be its control cabin. He thought he could see the pilot, but was not sure of this.

Karanda was the only one who noticed that, for all the flame and fume of its rocket motors, the strange white craft was climbing in absolute silence. This worried her very much and she poked a finger in her ear just in case the lightning had deafened her. But it hadn't.

As it reached Tim's height, the weird ship tilted heavily over out of its straight climb and drove towards the black walls of the storm valley.

Then, in an instant, it disappeared. One minute there was a spreading flower of red flame, the next there was nothing but cloud arms swirling dark against the retreating lightning.

'Funny,' said Sanchez to himself. 'I suppose there must have been a bank of cloud which I didn't see and it's flown behind it. Tim will know.'

'Back! Back!' the terrified voice of Mr Algeveer sounded in all their earphones. 'Abort excursion! Retract tow lines! Caravan retract tow lines! Return to base instantly!'

'Silly fuss,' thought Sanchez. 'The second half of the storm couldn't be much worse than the first half and the first half was great!'

But back on the caravan Mrs Algeveer had pressed the emergency switch to make the pressure clips reel in the safety lines. Like floundering fishes the five pilots were pulled back on to the balcony.

Mr Algeveer could hardly stand to get out of his harness. His jaw hung open and his whole face twitched nervously. Sigmond was at hand to help him.

'Chutar's Ride!' Mr Algeveer gasped. 'Chutar's

Ride! We've seen it! This is terrible. Did you see it?'

'I certainly saw something very strange,' Sigmond replied. 'Chutar's Ride is supposed to be seen just before something dreadful happens, isn't it?'

'Yes, yes,' Mr Algeveer agreed frantically. 'We must get back to the ground.'

He stumbled towards his stateroom. Karanda stood there hesitating whether to run after him. Thunder grumbled more loudly. The storm was coming back.

'My, my, oh my,' Uncle Algeveer, being plump had got stuck in his harness. 'This should have been avoided!'

'No one can blame you, dear.' Aunt Melinda was trying to help him out of the tangle of straps, but she was snapping her fingers so fast that she was getting him more mixed up.

'You must have had a very good view,' said Sigmond.

'Was that a ghost rocket ship?' asked Sanchez.

'Ghosts don't exist,' Tim said firmly. 'It was just a very old ship.'

'Did you hear any exhaust from its rockets?' Karanda asked fiercely.

'Come to think of it, no, I didn't.' Tim sounded subdued.

Sanchez felt a cold tickle down the back of his neck. He remembered Mr Algeveer's words: 'At times of disaster his great rocket ship is seen flaming through the skies with Chutar standing dead at the controls.'

'Dead at the controls,' Sanchez thought, and he was sure he had seen something in the light of that cabin.

'You will excuse us, please,' Mrs Algeveer had come back into the dining-room, trying to hide her worry. 'My husband has been very upset. He has asked your father to make for the space port of the Old Capital as quickly as possible on rocket power. We shall land in the early morning.'

A mile away they saw *Dragonfall*'s engines flare into power. She soared up and, with a gentle jerk, the caravan followed after in a smooth curve, out of the cloud valley where so much had happened. The storm fell away behind them, but it was still night.

'There's a cabin that Tim and Sanchez could have to sleep in tonight,' Sigmond suggested.

'Yes, of course, I'm so sorry,' Mrs Algeveer fluttered, 'and I do apologise for the upset.'

'That's quite all right,' Sanchez assured her. 'And we loved the stormride,' he told Karanda.

She gave him one of her saddest smiles and left.

As he showed them to their temporary bedroom Sigmond did not seem to want to talk about Chutar's Ride.

'When the sun comes up,' he said, 'everyone will see things differently. So good night!'

Left to themselves the two boys watched the stars for a minute or two. From a stateroom down the corridor they heard voices raised in argument. Then there was quiet.

'No fun tonight,' said Tim.

70

'What do you expect?' asked Sanchez. 'They were really frightened.'

'It's odd that they're so good at science and yet believe in ghosts,' said Tim. 'I thought scientists never believed in ghosts.'

'Well, we saw it too, didn't we?' asked Sanchez.

'We saw something,' Tim replied cautiously, 'but we don't know what it was. The air was charged with electricity so it could be some sort of freak mirage like you get over deserts. They say Lost Home is a desert planet.'

'Mmm!' said Sanchez, thinking of the lonely cabin light.

The two boys settled down for the night, but it was a while before either of them slept. Lightning still seemed to flash in Sanchez's eyes when he closed them. Jerk on his rug sighed with uneasy dreams.

In a long low trajectory *Dragonfall* and her tow coasted down to their landfall on a dying planet.

Chapter 5

No one woke in the caravan as *Dragonfall 5* came in at dawn to land at the space port of the Old Capital. Old Elias, still wearing his pyjamas, made a perfect landing, scowled at the salmon and orange glories of a desert sunrise and went straight back to bed again.

Sanchez woke several hours later, prodded Tim, hugged Jerk and then went out to the entrance port to smell the air. He loved first landings on new planets.

The space port was in the curve of a horseshoe of low hills and the hills were covered with the buildings of the Old Capital. Only to the south there were no houses, just open desert. But the red and brown of the desert sand seemed to have taken over the air because all the sky was in matching colours of pink, red and orange. Sanchez had been expecting this, because Sigmond had told them that on Lost Home the sunrises and sunsets lasted all day, as the sun, Khosro Khai, tried to shine through the desert dust. What surprised him were the buildings of the Old Capital. They were all of silvery grey wood, leaning and tottering against each other, winding uphill around narrow alleyways and breaking from time to time into little fretted towers and verandahs of carved timber.

As Tim joined him at the entry port a trumpet sounded far away over the hill, then another and another, so that all the air was filled with musical chords playing against each other.

'Eight o'clock,' said Tim.

'Is that all the trumpets mean?' Sanchez asked.

'Elephants like bells to tell the time and humans from Lost Home like trumpets,' Tim explained, 'so their clocks have bellows and pipes.'

'It's a good idea for a change,' said Sanchez. The Old Capital had fallen very quiet again after the last trumpet in the red morning. One or two cruise space ships for tourists were parked at the other side of the space port, but only one solitary figure seemed to be awake and that was an elephant trudging in their direction across the brown tarmac.

'I seem to know that figure,' said Tim.

'It's Sigmond with a basket. He's up early,' said Sanchez.

The two boys climbed down with Jerk to meet Sigmond.

'Couldn't you sleep?' Sigmond asked.

'No more than you,' Tim replied firmly. 'What have you been up to?'

'Oh, looking about to see what entertainments are on. The perfect waiter, you know!' said Sigmond in his usual airy style. 'And I've been to market to buy some new cereal. Humans love popcorn, probably because it explodes when you heat it!'

'All right, if you're in one of those moods,' said

Tim, and they left him to take his basket back to the caravan while they walked over to *Dragonfall*.

'Sometimes Sigmond does act a bit superior,' Sanchez admitted.

Old Elias and Big Mother had just got to the marmalade stage of breakfast.

'Ah, the wanderers return!' said Old Elias. 'What's been going on, eh! Have you been up to practical jokes scaring the wits out of the Algeveers?'

Tim went straight to the controls to look at the radar flight recorder while Sanchez told their mother and father all that had gone on the evening before. This was the first they had heard of the ghostly rocket ship and Chutar's Ride. They had both been in their bunks trying to sleep when the phantom ship had been sighted.

'Is it on the radar record?' Old Elias called to Tim who was poring over the screen.

'I know it happened at 10.41 hours exactly because I noted it on my watch,' Tim sounded worried. 'But there's not a trace of anything on this recorder screen.'

'There'd be a green radar trace on that if a mouse had gone by two miles away,' said Old Elias. 'It's very accurate.'

'I know,' Tim was unhappy. 'But there's nothing; yet we all saw it.'

'Humans that give you exploding cigars are not to be trusted,' Old Elias declared as he drank the last of his coffee. 'Practical joking is a disease and it gets a hold of you.'

'Good morning! Good morning!' Mr Algeveer's

voice boomed out of the intercom speaker. He sounded in one of his cheerful moods. Old Elias flicked on the visual link and the screen lit up to show all the Algeveers eating their breakfast in the caravan dining-room. Morween was dishing out peaches and honey.

'Congratulations, captain!' Mr Algeveer continued heartily. 'You have landed us safe and sound in the ancient home of my people.'

'What's this my boys have been telling me about a phantom space ship?' Old Elias interrupted rather rudely. 'You've been pulling another of your spoofing tricks, have you?'

Mr Algeveer glanced questioningly at Karanda, who gave him a stony glare. Then he broke into a very false laugh.

'That's it, captain, but I couldn't fool you, could I? Well, now we're safely on my native ground we're going to stay here a while. Last night I showed your boys how we play games. This afternoon I want to show you all how we play Plays. Uncle here has booked seats for all of us at the matinée. There's an Intergalactic Theatre Festival at our National Theatre — a wonderful building, I contributed to the costs myself, very high standards, a splendid show.

'What's the name of the play, my dear?' he turned to his wife who was eating solidly through her peaches and honey.

'*Hamlet*, dear,' she said, wiping her mouth. 'It's an Earth play, but it's being put on by a cast of elephants from Pine Home.'

'*Hamlet*, that's the name,' Mr Algeveer agreed

eagerly. 'It's a great play. I've often read it myself. I enjoy a good laugh at the theatre. Cast of elephants, eh! Ah well, it's an Intergalactic Festival and it takes all sorts to make a world. Starts at two o'clock sharp. We'll leave here at half past one.'

'Right you are, Commodore!' Old Elias replied, and the picture on the screen went dead.

In *Dragonfall*'s cabin the boys looked at each other in bewilderment.

'Pretending it was all a joke,' said Tim scornfully. 'He was so scared last night he could hardly stand up straight.'

'He's terrified of ghosts,' said Sanchez. 'He believes in them right up to his ears!'

'And he's in for a nasty shock at the theatre,' said Tim. 'I'll lay any money he's never read a word of *Hamlet*. He thinks its going to be funny and in fact everyone in it gets killed. Do you know how it starts?'

'Yes,' said Sanchez, 'with the ghost of a dead king walking at midnight on the battlements of an old castle!'

'I can't see Mr Algeveer rolling in the aisles with fun when that happens,' Old Elias exclaimed.

'I don't think,' Big Mother declared solemnly, 'that Mr Algeveer is altogether honest. People like that get what they deserve!'

All morning Tim, Sanchez, Sigmond and Karanda explored the Old Capital. It was a strange city. At first it was like going back in time: carved and crooked houses, fretwork parapets, wooden towers where trumpets played at every hour. Then

76

you began to notice how very few humans were really living there. Most of the houses were carefully preserved shells. Desert dust blew through the streets, sifting into the tourist shops where they sold fake antique muffs to keep the dust out of your ears.

'It's really just a museum,' said Sanchez.

'Full of ways to take your money,' agreed Karanda, eyeing the fortune tellers and pavement salesmen under the wooden arches.

'It's all built of wood,' said Tim, 'but I never see any trees.'

'That's why you never see them,' Sigmond explained. 'The old humans didn't like using stone, so they cut down all their forests and that's the real reason why Lost Home dried up. You need trees to make rain.'

'Now I'm getting gloomy,' said Sanchez.

Everyone had a light lunch together in the caravan and then the whole party of ten skimmed off in a fleet of hired hover cars to see the play. The hover cars wriggled up the narrow streets to the top of a hill and put them off in a wide square where a fountain pretended to squirt plastic water. Behind the fountain was a large modern building of pink concrete, looking very strange among the frail lovely buildings of the old city.

'Our National Theatre!' Mr Algeveer waved proudly. 'My own firm was honoured to give some of the money which built it.'

'Another of his expensive practical jokes,' Old Elias muttered.

The audience was flocking up the steps of the

National Theatre, but in front of the middle door, dividing the crowd on each side of her, sat an old lady elephant with snow-white fur. Her eyes were gazing wildly up into the sky, and cradled in her trunk she held something carefully wrapped in cloth.

'Who's that?' Mr Algeveer paused at the foot of the steps. 'Is she part of the show?'

'That's Mother Morrow,' Sigmond explained. 'She must have come over for the drama season. She is the most famous fortune teller on Pine Home. They say that everything she sees through her telechromic wires will come true before the end of a week.'

Mr Algeveer's face twitched and he pulled his black cloak around him.

'You mean I could ask her about that phantom ship and all those . . .'

'Father!' Karanda interrupted him furiously. 'These old ladies don't know any more about the future than you or I.'

As she said this Mother Morrow uttered a deep threatening sound in elephant language. It rang around the square and the other humans and elephants who were going up the stairs stopped to see what was going on.

The Minims popped up out of Sanchez's coat pockets where he had hidden them.

'What was that?' he whispered to them.

'She said "Blood",' reported the first.

'Nothing else,' said the second.

'Unfortunately,' said the third. He had had no work since leaving Pine Home.

'You see,' Karanda hissed at her father. 'You are making a show of us. Soon there will be more demonstrators.'

'And Mother Morrow is very expensive,' said Sigmond slyly, knowing how vain Mr Algeveer was about money. 'She won't speak a word for less than a hundred credits.'

Mr Algeveer drew from his pocket a small platinum bar and dropped it on the step in front of Mother Morrow. It fell with a thin ringing sound. More people gathered in a circle.

Slowly the old elephant rose to her feet. Her black robes swept the concrete steps and Tim noticed that when she turned to Mr Algeveer the platinum bar had gone. Out of her cloth-wrapped bundle she drew two shining tangles of meshed wire. These she pulled like gloves over Mr Algeveer's outstretched hands and long fingers. A third mesh of wires she pulled over her head and connected it by thin gold threads to the other two. All of this while she never gave Mr Algeveer a glance but continued to stare into the sky.

Somewhere in the city the trumpets began to sound for two o'clock. Almost a hundred of the curious were now gathered around the party from *Dragonfall*.

'I'd like to know . . .' began Mr Algeveer.

Abruptly Mother Morrow swung round to stare straight at the dim red disk of Khosro Khai. She screamed frighteningly, shaking in every limb, then called out deep low words in elephant language.

'Quick, keep translating!' Sanchez hissed.

'She sees fire, she sees air,' said the first Minim.

'She sees Chutar in the Heavens,' said the second.

'We don't know who he is,' pattered the third.

'Never mind, I do, keep going!' Sanchez pleaded.

'There is safety only in the desert,' the first Minim continued.

'By the falls of dust,' the second ended.

Mother Morrow fell to her knees and pointed upwards.

'She wants us to look,' said the third Minim unnecessarily.

Everyone automatically peered up in the direction

of the old lady's thick pointing finger. There was a gasp from the crowd. In mid-air a flame began to burn, consuming nothing. It grew and other flames were added to it until a whole furnace of them seemed to blaze far up above the crowd. Mother Morrow uttered a last word and suddenly all the flames were gone and there was just the dusky pink sky and the brutal shapes of the National Theatre.

'She said "Death",' the third Minim reported contentedly.

'What sort of show was that?' Big Mother asked suspiciously. 'Knowing the Algeveers I expect we'll get a pail of water over our heads next.'

'I think it's meant to be very serious,' said Sanchez. 'Did you see all those flames that I saw?'

'I thought I saw flames,' said Tim carefully.

Mr Algeveer turned away from Mother Morrow who now sat huddled on the steps. Looking very upset he tore the mesh gloves from his hands and dropped them in her lap, then strode up to the wide glass doors of the National Theatre. The rest followed him and were shown through carpeted rooms into a private box to the left of the stage in a big purple auditorium. The lights were just dimming for the play to begin and the *Dragonfall* party sat wherever there was a place. Sanchez found himself helping Uncle Algeveer into the seat next to him.

Sinsister music began to play, the air in the theatre grew very cold and Sanchez could smell a salty breath of the sea with perhaps a touch of woodsmoke behind it. The stage lights rose slightly to show the stage quite bare except for a number of

81

transparent glass boxes, each big enough to hold a man or a small elephant. All the glass boxes rested on the stage floor except for one which hung, dimly visible, in mid-air.

Silhouetted against the low stage lights Sanchez could make out Mr Algeveer in the seat in front of him. He looked restless and not at all himself. No wonder, poor fellow, thought Sanchez, if he had come here hoping for a good laugh.

'Is this your first time in the theatre?' a voice whispered in Sanchez's ear. It was Uncle Algeveer.

'Yes,' Sanchez whispered back.

'You'll find it very strange. I'll try and explain it to you.'

'Thank you,' said Sanchez. 'What are those glass boxes for?'

'Oh, the actors of course,' whispered Uncle Algeveer.

And indeed two elephants had just appeared in two of the glass boxes as if by magic and were talking to each other.

'They are sentries,' Uncle Algeveer explained. The play was in elephant language not in English. Something was worrying Sanchez. The two elephant actors did not seem to be looking straight at each other.

'Why do they stay in the boxes?' he whispered.

'Well, they can't very well get out!' Uncle Algeveer whispered back.

'Why not?'

'Because they're not here! They're not even on this planet. They're on the other one, but probably miles
82

away from each other. They're tele-projecting here in 3D from Pine Home!'

Two more boxes had been filled by two more actors; one of the first two had disappeared.

'Oh dear,' Uncle Algeveer whispered, 'my brother won't like this. One of them has seen a ghost earlier and he's brought his friend to see it. This is unfortunate after last night.'

'And Mother Morrow this afternoon,' Sanchez reminded him.

'Oh, you understood that, did you?'

'Of course,' Sanchez replied smugly.

The sinister music began again in low scraping chords. Mr Algeveer stirred restlessly in the front seat. A transparent white elephant appeared in the glass box suspended above the stage; it looked very disturbed, then vanished.

'That was the dead king,' Uncle Algeveer hissed. 'I knew this would be bad for my brother.'

Sanchez was more worried about the system.

'Why use tele-projection when you could have real actors?'

'This way you can have the very best actors. After all it is the National Theatre,' Uncle Algeveer explained. 'Here we gather the top stars together electronically.'

'But can they see each other?'

'Oh no!'

'So that's why they look cross-eyed. They don't know exactly where each other is standing?'

'I've told you. They're thousands of miles away from each other and literally millions of miles away from here. Yet by the miracles of modern science, we can sit here enjoying all the very best actors in one play.'

'But it doesn't look real!' Sanchez protested.

Since the ghost king had vanished the two remaining elephants were having a very long talk looking boss-eyed just over each other's left shoulder.

'The theatre isn't meant to be real. You don't want to pretend it's all true, do you?' Uncle Algeveer looked rather snootily. 'It's an art.'

Sanchez sat quietly for a minute trying to enjoy it. Mr Algeveer in front fidgeted in his seat and sighed.

'I'm afraid that the ghost king is going to come back again,' Uncle Algeveer muttered in Sanchez's ear. 'How tactless at such a time. There have been no jokes yet, no humour. Do you happen to know this play in English?'

'Yes.'

'Does it get any better?'

'No, much worse!'

'Oh dear! There'll be a row, and I booked the tickets,' Uncle Algeveer fretted. 'But that young elephant, Sigmond, who does the waiting, he told me it was a funny play!'

Horrid horn music and grim-sounding drums began to play again. The far-away actor who was playing the ghost king reappeared in his glass case hung in mid-air. This time he was pulling the most terrible faces and there were grinding metal noises as if swords were clashing. It was quite frightening even though the actor elephants were stuck in their tele-projection boxes. Sanchez saw Mr Algeveer grip the arms of his chair.

Finally a piercing cock crow sounded, so sharply that it seemed to be right in everyone's ear.

That was too much. Mr Algeveer staggered to his feet, blundered against his wife's seat and crashed his way towards the Exit, shouting, 'Give me some light!' at the top of his voice.

After a second of astonishment the whole party from *Dragonfall* got up and hurried after him. Safely several million miles away from the disturbance, the tele-projected actors went on acting. Several of the audience called out, 'Hush! Hush!' and 'Quiet!' Then the box door slammed shut and they were all out in the theatre looking dazed.

'Shortest play I ever saw!' Old Elias said and winked at Tim.

Mr Algeveer was leaning against a wall at the other side of the foyer. He was being comforted by an impressive elephant in a black cloak. Mrs Algeveer hurried towards him, and the black-coated elephant showed them both into an office with a grey marble door and a golden door handle.

'I told you that if he didn't like ghosts, he wouldn't like *Hamlet*,' said Tim.

'We knew he hadn't read it,' said Sanchez. 'Old show-off!'

'What a pity to miss the rest of it,' Uncle Algeveer complained gently. 'All those great actors and we hadn't even seen Hamlet himself. Sometime you must tell me about the part we missed.'

85

'We'll try,' said Tim, 'but it's very complicated and almost everyone dies in the end.'

'In that case perhaps it's as well we left,' the Uncle decided.

The Algeveers and the elephant in the black cloak came out of the grey marble door and beckoned them over. Mr Algeveer was looking better and Mrs Algeveer was smiling.

'There's been a change in plans,' she announced. 'My husband has been under strain and needs a complete rest, no space travel for a day or two,' she added firmly. 'Our good friend here,' she waved her hand towards the black-cloaked elephant who bowed deeply, 'has been kind enough to invite us out to stay at a guest house in the desert. He tells us that the peace there is quite remarkable.'

'Lovely old house,' the black-cloaked elephant interrupted in a deep melodious voice. 'Two thousand years old in the central wing, art treasures, beautiful scenery. It's called the Hall of the Falls of Dust.'

'I've rented the whole place for a week.' Mr Algeveer couldn't resist bringing money into it. The black-cloaked elephant looked rather pained. He gave a frozen smile and spoke to the *Dragonfall* family in his velvety voice.

'And how did you enjoy the first scene of our play?'

'It smelt nice,' Tim said.

The elephant smirked and twitched back his cloak.

'Yes, I thought that was a good idea myself,' he said. 'No one else has thought of trying to make a Shakespeare play smell right. It is a shame you didn't stay for the duel scene when there is all that blood around. We manage some very interesting effects!'

'But we thought the production was silly because none of the characters could get at each other,' said Sanchez, 'stuck in those electronic boxes.'

'The characters were not meant to "get at each other",' said the impressive elephant stonily, 'and I was the producer!'

In an awkward silence he huffed back into his office and clashed the marble door behind him.

'That was the great producer, Barromane Barrouk,' Mrs Algeveer explained nervously. 'He is running the whole International Festival of Plays at this theatre. He hates being criticised.'

'Well, he's in the wrong job,' said Tim.

'And I still think those tele-projection boxes were silly,' said Sanchez.

'You boys have got something there,' Mr Algeveer agreed, 'I thought the whole play was very unhealthy. But now I want you all to come off with me and get some wholesome desert air. We're going to have a great time again!'

'You're taking everyone, are you?' Uncle Algeveer asked. Tim looked sharply at him because he sounded so disturbed. 'I wonder,' Uncle continued, 'if the Hall of the Falls of Dust is quite the place for children?'

'Why not?' Mr Algeveer sounded firm. 'We'll have a party. Fun and games and laughter, that's what I need after all this phantom nonsense!'

'*Dragonfall 5* can land anywhere and the boys will be sleeping with us. They won't get in your way,' Big Mother assured them.

Mr Algeveer's face twitched and he grabbed at the wall for support.

'Oh, we won't be going in *Dragonfall*,' he said quickly, 'not by air at all! Oh dear no! Not for a few days in any case. I shall take you all in a Sand Bat. Yes, that will be much more soothing. I'll hire a Sand Bat Attack Manta Ray Super de Luxe Plus Coupe.' The name seemed to soothe him. 'It has an air conditioned force field with sun filters, you'll enjoy that. Sunbathing at a hundred miles an hour and no dust.'

'Father!' Karanda's stormy voice cut in on his rush of words. 'Father! Why are you going to this place? What do you know about it? Why can't we go storm riding again? That was what you promised.'

'Storm riding!' Mr Algeveer gasped. 'Oh no, my dear! No more space flights, not for a little while. Not until the danger is over. Feet firmly on dry land, that's the thing.'

'Just because an old elephant woman sees flames in the air,' Karanda was coldly furious, 'all our holiday is spoilt.'

'Only for a week, my dear,' Mr Algeveer pleaded. 'And this Hall of the Falls of Dust is hundreds of miles from any demonstrators.'

'It is a famous guest house,' Sigmond put in. 'Lots of film stars have stayed there and there was a TV feature on it in a Stately Homes series.'

'Peace and quiet is what we need,' Mrs Algeveer insisted.

'Absolute rest,' echoed the Aunt.

'Miles from anywhere,' ended the Uncle doubtfully. 'Three hundred and fifty miles from the next house, so I believe.'

'Don't feel that you have to take us,' said Big Mother. '*Dragonfall 5* can easily pick up another set of guests.'

'Oh please, no!' Mr Algeveer suddenly looked white and ill. 'I still want you, but I want you to stay on the ground. After all, I've hired you. Karanda enjoys company of her own age.'

'Though she may not always show it,' he added hastily after a glare from his daughter.

'You take Tim and Sanchez then,' Big Mother decided. 'Their father and I will stay behind and give *Dragonfall* a spring cleaning.'

'But you'll stay on the ground, no take-offs?' Mr Algeveer insisted.

'No take-offs,' Big Mother agreed.

'Now let's get back,' said Mr Algeveer, managing his first smile for some time. 'I don't like the atmosphere of this place. A little culture goes too far.'

The hover taxis were not expecting them so soon and they had to walk back down the narrow dusty ways in the afternoon heat. A few demonstrators, some human and some elephant, but all very young, were gathering with banners at the space-port gate; but these were expecting to shout at hover cars and they did not notice as the Algeveers and

89

Dragonfallers slipped through. Karanda muttered rude words under her breath.

'You see, my dear,' her mother told her, 'for peace and quiet we need to get miles away.'

Back in *Dragonfall*, Sanchez and the Minims told Tim, Big Mother and Old Elias what Mother Morrow had said about seeing fire in the air and seeking safety at the Falls of Dust.

'Then just a few minutes later Mr Algeveer gets invited to stay at a place called the Hall of the Falls of Dust. That's too much of a chance for me to believe in,' said Tim. 'Someone is pushing us and I don't like it.'

'Obviously Mr Algeveer thinks that if he goes anywhere in *Dragonfall* he'll crash in flames,' said Sanchez.

They all looked at each other and Old Elias patted the hull. The idea of *Dragonfall 5* crashing in flames was very bad.

'Well,' Big Mother decided, 'someone has made him think that and he's paying us good money, so if he says "stay grounded", we'll stay grounded. But we're responsible for him. I want you boys to keep your eyes wide open when you get to these Halls of Dust. It doesn't sound like a nice clean guest house to me. The first sign of trouble, radio to us on the inter-com.'

'They won't be able to,' Old Elias said flatly. There is too much fine dust in the atmosphere of this planet for ordinary radio waves. Once they're there, they'll be on their own!'

This worrying thought was broken by the piercing

blast of a five-note electric horn. Sanchez rushed to the door.

'Wow!' he cried. 'It's a Super de Luxe Plus Coupe all right!'

It was the promised Sand Bat with Mr Algeveer already at the controls and his family lounging on the deck under the air-conditioned, sun-filtered force field. The Bat wobbled towards them from the caravan with flashes of static electricity jumping the few inches between its flat keel and the ground. Sand Bats can circle a whole planet without refuelling because they pick up their power from electricity created by sand rubbing on sand.

This one was outsize. It was as big as four motor-coaches pressed together, but it was built low and flat and rakish, shaped more like a flying squirrel than a bat. The flexible wings down its two long sides bent and wriggled all the time as they picked up current. The main fuselage was orange with chromium strips. There were fourteen headlamps in the front and ten at the back.

'All aboard!' Mr Algeveer called out heartily. 'Join our flying drawing-room.' He was standing in the prow holding a two-foot steering tiller shaped like a leaping dragon. All the terrors of ghosts and theatres were far behind him.

A retractable arm shaped like a cockle shell and padded with mauve carpet came humming out to meet them. The boys, Jerk, the Minims and their luggage piled into the shell to be carried over the flexible wings and set down on the deck. Not that 'deck' was the right word. Mr Algeveer had called it a flying

91

drawing-room and that was what it looked like. There was a three-piece suite, loungers, armchairs, tables and a cocktail cabinet, all looking as if they were in the open air with no roof, but all actually safe from wind and dust under the force field.

Karanda was slumped in a lounger reading a book. Mrs Algeveer was playing cards with Uncle and Aunt. Morween was mixing fruit juices and Sigmond was waiting with tall glasses on a tray to serve everyone.

'Every comfort here,' he said, and winked at Sanchez as he passed him a glass.

With a gentle electric hum and a fanfare from its horns the Sand Bat rose a few inches and then made off at a stately pace for the open desert. Big Mother waved once, then went back in to begin her spring cleaning. Old Elias cleaned his pipe and watched until the Sand Bat was lost on the dusty horizon.

Chapter 6

At first Tim and Sanchez leant out against the force field, sipping their drinks and watching the desert race away past the stern of the Sand Bat. Karanda joined them for a while; she was bored with her book, and they tried playing I Spy. But almost everything they could think of spying began with an S, like sand and stone and sky. Sanchez tried varying it by things like rock or pebble or rubble, but Karanda said that was cheating so they had a little quarrel and stopped.

Picnic tea was a break. They sat on sofas and armchair arms nibbling titbits and snacks, all the while feeling a little ridiculous to be sitting there in comfort while they rippled at full tilt across a howling wilderness. Mr Algeveer was happy again and he sang as he drove the Sand Bat at a steady eighty miles an hour. Hour after hour they travelled on over windworn rocks, soft white gypsum sands and plains of gravel. Sometimes they passed low hills, sometimes they crossed the valleys of dead rivers, but in all that time they never saw a house or any living thing. Pop music played loudly all the time and Mr Algeveer often sounded his fanfare horn, but it was to cheer them up, not to warn anyone that they were coming.

'No wonder Chutar was so keen to get to the other planet,' said Sanchez. 'I shouldn't think it rained here once in a year.'

'Less than that,' said Tim. 'Now they're just using up the water that's stored under the ground. Soon it will all be gone.'

'It seems an odd place to be going for a rest cure.' Sanchez said.

'Particularly if you're inclined to gloomy fits,' Tim agreed.

'Karanda!' Sanchez called. 'Who is running this luxury hotel we're going to, humans or elephants?'

Karanda glanced at Uncle Algeveer who looked nervously at his brother, but Mr Algeveer was standing at the tiller well out of hearing range.

'I wouldn't call it a luxury hotel,' said Uncle carefully. 'Not from what I hear. It's run almost single-handed by a lady cousin of the great producer, Barromane Barrouk, whom we were lucky enough to meet just now at the theatre. She is called Annomane Barrouk and she is, of course, an elephant. I know nothing else about her.'

'Considering that this was originally a human planet,' said Tim, 'we do seem to get mixed up with a surprising number of elephants.'

Karanda, who was listening, frowned. Uncle shrugged his shoulders helplessly.

'I sometimes feel the same, but my brother is in charge and elephants are a very warm-hearted helpful race.'

94

'Yes, we found that,' Tim said meaningfully. 'That's why we're here now on a bumpy journey to nowhere, miles from help if anything bad happens.'

The sun was just beginning to set in swirls of brown and purple when Uncle Algeveer pointed ahead.

'You see there. At the end of that line of cliffs and below the red hills.'

'Isn't there some sort of ruin?' Sanchez peered in the dim light.

'It may look like a ruin, indeed it may be a ruin,' Uncle Algeveer liked to be precise, 'but I believe that we are looking at the Hall of the Falls of Dust.'

Mr Algeveer too had seen the Hall and he shouted to his family, 'Journey's end and a good dinner!'

The Sand Bat hissed across a wide river of dust, wobbled up a stony slope and swung in a side-slipping curve towards the buildings on the cliff. The rock walls rose up a hundred feet. All along the crest, clinging to every dip and pinnacle of the rock, was a line of wooden towers and red stone halls.

'It's huge!' said Sanchez.

'Soft beds for everyone!' Mr Algeveer was still cheerful.

The Hall of the Falls of Dust was like a cross between a castle and a town. Barromane Barrouk had said at the theatre that parts of the Hall were two thousand years old. In the wild sunset light, with its blind and twisted windows, crazy hanging galleries and gaping door, the boys could believe that it was as old as the hills on which it grew.

The Sand Bat shivered to a halt, grinding a little

on the rocks. Then the complete silence of the place settled down on them.

'Do we knock the door, father, or call up a battering ram?' Karanda asked sarcastically.

'Annomane Barrouk will be here in a minute, my dear,' Mr Algeveer replied patiently, but Tim noticed his fingers working fretfully on the tiller.

They waited one minute. Then they waited five. Still no one came. The silence was beginning to make everyone nervous.

'There's a cat,' said Sanchez.

Jerk growled. A little grey cat face was looking down at them from a crumbling parapet. It vanished. The sun had gone and twilight was closing quickly.

It was Mrs Algeveer who finally got them moving.

'We'd better make a start with the luggage,' she said, 'or we'll be here all night.'

Sigmond set the retracting arm in motion and soon the whole party was scrambling up a zigzag path of shale towards the great door. With the darkness growing and all the luggage to carry it was not an easy climb, and there was some puffing and panting by the time they reached the shadows of the porch.

'Not a single step!' said Tim indignantly. 'You'd think someone didn't want people to get here.'

'And not a single light,' said Sanchez.

'It is really too bad!' said the Uncle.

As if someone had heard them, and perhaps someone had, at that very moment a pale silvery light went on in all the odd, up and down, hole and corner windows of the sprawling castle. It was as if moonlight were shining out from inside it.

'Ah!' Mr Algeveer sighed with relief.

Through the great door they could see a long raftered hall with steps at the far end, and down the steps, holding a small bright light, a tall female elephant was stepping. As she began the walk along the hall they could see that she was wearing a grey dress down to the ground. Little figures hurried around her feet, slinking and dodging as she walked.

'More cats!' said Sanchez. Jerk drew back his ears bristling and Sanchez bent down to hold him in case he did something unfortunate. The tall female elephant reached the door and stood there without saying anything.

'Am I speaking to Annomane Barrouk?' Mr Algeveer asked very formally.

The tall elephant glanced at him vaguely. It was as if he were not quite there and she had forgotten something, like half a pound of butter. Then her eyes fell on Sanchez holding Jerk, and a smile lit up her face.

'You love animals,' she declared in a low deep voice, 'so you cannot be wholly bad! Has your dog had food and water?'

'I think so,' said Sanchez, remembering how Jerk had spent the last few hours begging for bits in Morween's kitchen corner.

'Animals suffer terribly here from thirst, you know,' the tall elephant continued. 'Always remember that and try to make his short life happy, as I try with my kitties.'

'Eeyow,' said the kitties and scrambled up her dress, scratching and tearing their way so that she could cradle an armful of them.

The Algeveers were quite silenced by all this; they stood there in a weary half circle staring at the cats. And the cats stared back at them. Far away in some lonely tower a trumpet clock blew for eleven o'clock.

'Whatever was Cousin Barromane thinking of to send you here at this time of night?' the elephant asked.

'Isn't this a hotel?' Mr Algeveer faltered. 'I thought I'd rented it for a week.'

'Hotel!' Annomane's voice was full of disgust. 'Hotel! Sometime in the future we hope to turn it into a haven of rest for animals and for owners who

99

are sensitive to the spiritual powers that are so strong here. But it will never be a hotel!'

'Spiritual powers?' Mr Algeveer repeated.

'You don't mean that this place is haunted, do you?' Uncle asked.

'For two thousand years people have lived here,' Annomane's voice went very low, 'so I never feel alone!'

'How's that?' Mr Algeveer rapped nervously.

'Sometimes I hear the swish of a dress round a corner, or laughter in an empty room, or perhaps music from a broken flute in a deserted tower; lovely harmless sounds,' Annomane ended soothingly.

'You mean there're ghosts here?' Mr Algeveer's face was twitching again.

'At night of course you might see darker things if you looked for them. For myself I keep to certain rooms where the powers are kindly. It does not do to meddle with evil forces.'

'That settles it,' Mr Algeveer gasped. 'We're all going back now!'

'That is impossible,' Annomane looked through him gently. 'Listen, the Falls of Dust have begun their nightly flow.'

To the left, where the cliff line ended with a hanging tower, a strange rustling sound had begun. It increased as they listened, like thunder heard through cotton wool.

'It flows each night from sunset to sunrise,' Annomane smiled as she spoke. 'While it flows the river of dust which you have just crossed becomes a raging torrent impossible to pass. Everywhere else there are the cliffs. You must spend the night here. Your dog is very welcome.'

'At sunrise I'll be waiting to go,' Mr Algeveer promised.

'Come in from the dark night,' Annomane commanded. 'This house has five hundred rooms, you must each find one where the spiritual forces suit you.'

As they began to follow her into the first hall, Sanchez saw something carved above the inner door.

'Look!' he gasped.

'What?' Mr Algeveer snapped in nervous alarm.

'Up there,' Sanchez pointed, 'carved on the shield. It's a black sword brandished by a black arm. That's Chutar's crest. I saw it painted on the phantom space ship!'

'He's right,' Karanda confirmed. 'I saw it too.'

'Oh dear, oh dear,' the Uncle muttered.

Annomane turned halfway down the hall.

'But didn't you know?' she asked. 'Surely Barromane told you!'

'He told us we'd get absolute peace and quiet here,' Mrs Algeveer replied indignantly. She was half carrying her husband by this time.

'Yes, peace and quiet,' the Aunt added.

'This house was owned nine hundred years ago by Chutar's elder brother Ingar,' Annomane ignored the interruptions. 'He too was a great inventor, a noble soul.' She paused. 'He perished before his brother.'

'How?' asked the Uncle faintly.

'Terribly.' Annomane's voice sank low and one of her hands closed over a cat's face. 'He experimented with the electrical transmission of matter, hoping to escape from this dying planet. He built one transmitter in the highest tower here and entered it himself, intending to be transported by electric currents to the Second Transmitter deep in the cellar. The current was switched on.'

'Did he reach the Second Transmitter?' Tim asked, since Annomane seemed to have forgotten them. She rolled her eyes wearily.

'Yes, but hideously deformed. He died within the hour and was buried by night. They say his own wife did not recognise him.'

Mr Algeveer gave a little moan and was helped to a wooden bench.

'The Second Transmitter is still shown to interested tourists.' Annomane sounded as if she would like to show it to them. 'But the first transmitter was destroyed by Ingar's wife with an axe!'

'Good,' said Sanchez. 'So we won't step into it by accident.'

'Now,' Annomane waved to the stairs that wound up into the silvery shadows, 'go up and choose bedrooms for yourselves. Remember, the aura should be just right! I must go to prepare food for my kitties and your fine dog. Afterwards I suppose you would like a meal yourselves.'

She shook her head and drifted off up the stairs ahead of them.

'Maybe I could just sit here and look after the luggage,' Aunt Melinda suggested. She was smiling

102

bravely, but she had begun to snap her fingers again, which was always a nervous sign.

'Wouldn't it be better if we all kept together?' asked the Uncle.

'Quite the wisest thing,' Mrs Algeveer agreed. 'And I want to know exactly where I'm sleeping in this place.'

'This is rather exciting,' said Sanchez. 'I've never been to a hotel before where you could choose your own room.'

'Not a hotel,' Tim mimicked, 'a haven of rest!'

'For kitties!' Sanchez added. They both collapsed in helpless giggles. Karanda almost joined them, but then she remembered how responsible she was, so she made her face serious again and marched off down a dark corridor. After dithering a little the Algeveers chose the broadest, brightest corridor. Jerk sniffed the air and decided to stay where he was and watch out for cats, so Tim and Sanchez set out by themselves down a narrow passage. Iron masks hung on the walls and large cupboards half blocked the way. There were little steps up and down at every bend.

'What's that smell?' Tim asked.

'Burnt herbs.' Sanchez held up a metal bowl full of ashes. 'That will be Annomane for sure. She probably spends half the day at it.'

'How about this room?' Tim tried a door and found that it swung open easily.

'Is the aura right?' Sanchez asked, and they had another fit of laughing.

'Really, you know,' said Tim, 'if someone had just

set out to drive Mr Algeveer out of his mind they couldn't have done better than this place.'

'Or the whole holiday cruise for that matter,' Sanchez added. 'Just think, there've been demonstrations, phantom space ships, frightening fortune tellers, *Hamlet*'s ghosts and now this spook castle.'

'But I like the room,' said Tim.

It was large with peaked rafters, the cupboards and shelves were of bleached silvery wood. As Tim walked over to the window the floorboards creaked almost in a musical tune. The bed hung on chains from the ceiling.

'And look at the view!'

Sanchez came over to see. Pine Home, the twin planet, was high in the sky, shedding a green light over the desert. Just below their window a lake of dust was shifting forwards to pour in muffled thunder over the great falls. From out of sight below them the gypsum dust came surging up again in a cloud to make faint rainbows in the light.

'If it weren't for Annomane,' Tim began, 'this place would be a wonderful . . .'

'Aahh! aaaah!'

Two blood curdling screams sounded from away in the warren of corridors and rooms.

'It's Mr Algeveer! We were supposed to keep an eye on him. Quickly!' Tim yelled. The two boys blundered out of the room and began frantically searching down the twisting corridors, stumbling down steps and crashing into massive furniture. The sound of angry voices led them into a broad passageway. Mr Algeveer was slumped in a three-legged

chair opposite an open doorway. Mrs Algeveer and
the Uncle were glancing nervously from Mr Algeveer to the door.

'Shut it!' he shouted as the boys turned the corner.
'Shut it or they'll get out! They'll be everywhere!'

'What is it? What's wrong?' the boys asked.

'My poor Algeveer. This is a dreadful place,' Mrs
Algeveer wailed.

'That elephant woman, she's mad,' Mr Algeveer
gasped. 'She told us to look around, to choose a
room for ourselves, and what happened?'

'Yes, yes,' Sanchez urged him on.

Mr Algeveer loosened his collar, sat up and spoke
more quietly.

'Well, to be frank I was terrified. I have had, as
you know, a very bad time of late. So I walked along
this corridor, afraid to open any of the doors.'

'I can understand that,' said the Uncle. 'I still
haven't opened one and now I'm not going to.'

'Finally,' Mr Algeveer continued, 'my dear wife
said that we had to sleep somewhere so I plucked
up courage and opened that.' He pointed across to
the open door. 'It's full of spiders. Full to bursting
point. Spiders!'

He fell back again with his eyes shut.

'He's right!' Tim peered cautiously. The room was
a tangled mass of thick spider's webs. Tiny lights of
spiders' eyes shone from its darkest corners and over
all the webs was a horrid movement of fat creepy
bodies.

'How dare you?' Annomane's angry voice
stormed. No one had heard her padding up.

105

'But look,' the Uncle spluttered, 'this room is full of spiders!'

'And what harm have they done you? There are five hundred rooms in this house and is even one of them to be denied to these poor creatures as a haven?' Annomane demanded. 'You come here screeching and disturbing them. Pretty dears,' she said soothingly to the spiders. 'That door shall be locked tomorrow.'

'They should be swept away!' Mrs Algeveer declared. 'They might get out and suffocate people in their sleep. Anything could happen.'

'Have you seen one other spider's web anywhere in this house?' Annomane asked.

Everyone tried to remember.

'No, you haven't, nor will you ever! This room is my spiders' only nest. Here they can live out their peaceful life span. But what do you know or care about peace?' Annomane swung round and glared at Mr Algeveer. 'You with your wicked weapons that can destroy whole planets at the touch of a switch. No spider is safe from you!'

Mr Algeveer started at this and exchanged a worried glance with the Uncle.

'But while you are in my house you will destroy nothing,' Annomane ended and swung off down the corridor.

'She knows about our A.U. Destructor,' the Uncle whispered.

'Who doesn't?' Mr Algeveer groaned despairingly. 'If only I had never thought of the thing. Since I invented it everything has gone badly.'

106

'Well,' said the Uncle, 'you know what I've advised you to do!'

But the boys did not find out what the Uncle's advice had been for just then Karanda came running down the corridor and of course she had to be shown the spiders.

For a minute she gazed through the door at them as they crept and rustled.

'That's a great idea!' she breathed. 'Much more fun than keeping cats or dogs. Could I keep some at home, Father? We've got plenty of spare rooms.'

'We must talk it over, my dear,' said Mr Algeveer faintly.

'When we are all a little stronger,' Mrs Algeveer explained. 'Let us go downstairs and see if Annomane has finished feeding her cats and left a little for us?'

Down below Annomane Barrouk was seated at the head of a long table in a dining-room where a hundred warriors could have feasted. Her cats were standing on the table in front of her, gobbling greedily from a silver bowl brimming with food. Jerk was sitting on the floor watching them. Every so often one of the cats would pull a bit out of the bowl and mess about with it on the polished table. Jerk growled again. He was never allowed to stand on a table or make messes.

'Sit down,' Annomane invited them with a tired wave of her trunk. 'There is a bowl of parched grain for each of you and in that jug will find a real treat: the coldest purest mineral water in all Lost Home.

107

Savour every drop of it. It comes from a spring deep below the Hall of the Falls of Dust.'

The grain in their bowls was so parched that you would have needed a set of cast-iron teeth to chew it, but they were saved from complaining because at that moment Sigmond came in from outside balancing four trays loaded with good things.

'Morween has been busy in her kitchen corner,' he whispered as he tactfully slipped these new plates on to the table. He left a dish of curdled cream and pineapple purée in front of Annomane, but she pushed it scornfully aside and crunched at her parched grain.

It was a very subdued meal. Something was wrong which no one could quite be sure about. There was very little conversation. After a last sip of her special mineral water Annomane made an announcement.

'Cousin Barromane will be here soon.'

'Really, that's good of him,' the Uncle said politely.

'How is he travelling?' Mr Algeveer asked eagerly.

'In his usual anti-grav jet, I suppose,' Annomane replied.

'Saved!' Mr Algeveer exclaimed. 'We can travel back in it to the Old Capital immediately.

'It is a one-man anti-grav,' Annomane told him crushingly.

Silence fell again, broken only by eating noises and the cats miaowing at each other. The dining-room was not an easy eating place. Its walls were lined with paintings of fierce warriors and their grumpy-looking wives. All these portraits except the very earliest were painted in 3D with moving eyes, so that whenever Sanchez looked up from his food there was a savage face glaring and winking at him.

To take his mind off these he tried counting the cats, but even this was hard. They were all grey with light faces and dark eyes, and they kept snaking confusingly about each other as they ate or as Annomane fondled them. Finally he asked, 'How many cats are there, please?'

Annomane smiled for the first time in the meal.

'My kitties?' she said, running her hands fiercely over them so that they all squawled and miaowed. 'There are five of them.'

'Only five!' Sanchez would have guessed about fifteen.

'Only five, the lithe, lovely beauties. They are called Tiggerbits, Sketchybits, Lillibits, Bumperbits and Naughtybits,' she told him proudly.

'And which is your favourite?' Sanchez asked, thinking there was no harm in being pleasant.

'This one,' Annomane snatched up the cat with the palest head. 'This is Naughtybits. He is my treasure and I take him everywhere.'

'Greetings, cousin, and greetings, kitties all!' a splendid mellow voice boomed out from a balcony at the end of the dining-room. It was Barromane Barrouk himself. This time he was wearing a purple cloak lined with scarlet silk. He bowed with twiddling movements of both hands.

'Cousin Barromane!' Annomane was on her feet and beaming, cats went scattering everywhere. 'I didn't hear you coming.'

109

'I landed on the North Tower in my latest super-silenced 4 KO model jet,' Barromane replied. 'There was barely a whisper of exhaust gases.'

'Is there room for a passenger?' Mr Algeveer asked plaintively.

'Our guest is weary of his stay already,' Annomane told her cousin.

'What's this?' Barromane gave a great rolling laugh, perfectly rounded. 'Not tired already of the Falls of Dust! Why, what can you have learned at this short space of its sweet spiritual influences and its kindly calm?'

'One room's full of spiders!' Mrs Algeveer called angrily.

'The cellars are alive with ghosts!' Mr Algeveer spluttered.

'And not a decent salad to be had in the house,' said Uncle mildly.

'Ghosts, no!' Barromane boomed back. 'But gentle spiritual effluences, perhaps, yes. Stay, I beseech you, and savour them with me.'

In one bound he had leaped down from the balcony and was striding towards them smiling and kissing hands. He kissed his cousin's hand, he kissed Mrs Algeveer's hand and then he was just about to kiss the Uncle's when he stopped and looked in surprise.

'Now where is the pretty Aunt Melinda?' he asked.

For several seconds no one said anything, because up to that time no one had noticed that the Aunt was missing, not even the Uncle. That had been the wrong thing disturbing them all ever since the meal began.

'My poor wife, where is she?' the Uncle sat down and looked vaguely under the table.

'Not down there, we may be sure!' Annomane said witheringly. 'Is she usually late for meals?'

'Never,' said the Uncle firmly.

They all looked at each other for a moment, the silence and the shadows of the great house hung about them. Suddenly Mrs Algeveer burst into noisy tears.

'She's gone,' she cried. 'Poor Melinda has gone! We'll never see her again. It's this terrible place. Something dreadful has taken her. I can feel it in my bones!'

'Gently there, gently!' Barromane interrupted in his most syrupy voice. 'Aunt Melinda can come to no harm in this restful house. Perhaps she was tired by her journey and has fallen asleep somewhere. We must be calm. Come now. Who saw her last?'

He managed to make this question sound quite sinister. The Uncle shuffled his feet and stood up.

'I suppose I did,' he said.

'And where, pray, was that?' Barromane demanded.

'In a corridor somewhere,' the Uncle faltered.

'You left poor Melinda in a corridor,' Barromane repeated accusingly. 'Was that wise?'

'I heard my brother cry out,' the Uncle explained unhappily, 'so I just ran back to see what was happening. Melinda must have sat down. I never thought . . .'

111

'You never thought,' repeated Barromane again.

Everyone looked at the Uncle, who looked very wretched.

> *'A noble soul will never cower*
> *Take courage at the darkest hour,'*

a familiar voice sounded from the dark doorway. It was Morween coming up from the Sand Bat with more trays of food.

> *'Cheer up your hearts and never mind*
> *For if you search you're sure to find,'*

she continued as she set down the trays.

'How right you are.' Barromane suddenly sprang into action. 'We must divide and search every room in the house. She may be wandering somewhere lost in the cellars.'

'The cellars, cousin Barromane, we must hope she did not enter the cellars,' Annomane's voice quivered gloomily.

'Morween and I will search the west wing,' Sigmond burst in to stop Mr Algeveer asking upsetting questions about the cellars. 'Mr and Mrs Algeveer will search the East Wing.'

'I will sit here and absorb the spiritual vibrations,' Annomane said. 'Perhaps I can help poor Melinda best in that way. She may be beyond normal aid.'

'Yes,' Sigmond agreed hurriedly. 'Barromane will search the State Apartments and the Uncle can search the Towers. Tim, Sanchez and Karanda can look in the North Wing.'

'Tim and Sanchez can search the North Wing,' Karanda cut in, 'but I shall search the cellars, and any spiritual vibrations that get in my way had better hang on tight to their auras!'

She got up, glared at everyone defiantly, then marched off to where a flight of steps led down under an archway. Her small figure with bobbed hair and smartly cut black suit went down into the dark.

'Rather her than me,' said Sanchez admiringly.

'A girl with a mind of her own,' said Barromane.

'We must begin our search, anything may have happened,' the Uncle wailed. 'There is no time to lose.'

They went as Sigmond had divided them. Tim and Sanchez were to search the North Wing. They climbed upstairs, passed the spider room again and made their way around the twisting passages, trying every room and cupboard. Even Tim found it eerie. There was always just enough of the dim silver light for them to see where they were going, but in between the lighted stretches were corridors of shade, and the rooms they searched had heavy carved furniture where anything could be lurking. The voices of the other searchers were soon lost and there was only the soft muffled roar of the Falls of Dust and the creaking sounds you hear in all old houses.

'What about secret passages?' Sanchez suggested. 'Ought we to be tapping the walls?'

'Best to go quietly,' Tim whispered. 'Then we may surprise whoever has got her.'

'You think that's what's happened?' Sanchez

asked anxiously. 'You think something has grabbed her?'

'Well, she wouldn't hide away of her own accord, would she?' Tim sounded confident. 'Not with dinner around.'

'Do you think it's Barromane Barrouk who has shut her up somewhere?' Sanchez suggested. 'We didn't hear him land his super-silenced 4KO antigrav jet, and I wouldn't trust him very far.'

'I wouldn't trust any of them,' Tim replied, looking into yet another dark vaulted room. 'They're all up to something we only half understand.'

'Have you noticed something about Morween?' Sanchez asked as he rummaged in the bottom of a huge carved chest.

'The way she works?' Tim suggested, flapping old tapestries away from the wall.

'No, the way she talks,' Sanchez went on. 'Doesn't it remind you a little of the way someone else talks?'

'Annomane, you mean!' Tim paused in the search. 'Perhaps you've got something there. They are both loopy in rather the same way. Are you suggesting that they're related?'

'Linked anyway,' Sanchez continued. 'All this hope and peace and quiet stuff. I think that they're both . . .'

'Listen!' Tim hissed.

Far away and below them came the sound of a blaster bolt.

'Low-power personal blaster on half-charge paralysis ray by the sound of it.' Tim cocked his head to listen again. Another bolt and then another followed the first. There was a faint quiver in the foundations of the house and the sound of falling stones. Then faintly a shout of, 'Father!'

'It's Karanda in the cellar,' said Tim. 'Something's after her!'

'More likely she's after something,' Sanchez corrected him.

Once more they went hurrying down the halls and passages, taking the steps three and four at a time. They reached the dining-room as the other searchers came in panting and puffing. Annomane was still seated at the table with her cats. But now she was feeding the titbits to Jerk.

'Where is Karanda?' Mr Algeveer demanded. 'We heard three blaster bolts!'

'This house is full of noises,' Annomane replied calmly. 'They are echoes of the long dead past. I hardly notice them.'

'Long dead past be bothered!' Karanda's voice rang out hollowly. 'That was me!'

She came climbing up the steps into the light, covered with dust and swinging a small blaster in her right hand. She threw the blaster on to the table where it sizzled sharply in a bowl of shredded fish salad.

'My child,' Mr Algeveer hurried towards her, 'what has happened to you?'

'I knocked the roof down,' said Karanda calmly.

'This is an ancient monument. You had no right –' Annomane began.

'Nobody fools around with me, ancient monument or otherwise,' Karanda sat down. Sanchez thought she was probably more shaken than she wanted them to know.

'Tell us what happened, my child,' Mrs Algeveer sat down and put her arm around Karanda's shoulder. Karanda shrugged her away, picked up a stick of celery and began to crunch it.

'I went down into the cellars to see what there was to get all worked up about,' she explained between munches. 'It was dark and I couldn't see much, then I heard this chomping noise: chomp, chomp, chomp with a bit of a stumble in it, a long way off at first but getting near, as if something was following me.'

'Ingar's ghost,' breathed Annomane. 'After he came out of the Second Transmitter his legs were fitted on backwards – he limped!'

'It was kind of scarey if you get scared,' Karanda admitted, 'but I don't! Anyway it was getting nearer and I'd reached this Second Transmitter place, when suddenly it all lit up.'

'The electrical circuits perished many hundred years ago,' Annomane interrupted in her usual doomladen tones. 'There could be no lights.'

'I saw lights,' Karanda insisted, 'so I turned round and coming up the passage after me I could just see this ugly-looking shape.'

'My poor child!' Mr Algeveer collapsed again on to a bench. 'What did you do?'

'Gave it a bolt on my blaster at half-power paralysis ray,' Karanda replied with a glint in her eye. 'That's what brought the ceiling down!'

'Carrying weapons of destruction at your age,' Annomane reproved her.

'Yes, I should learn to shoot straight,' Karanda agreed. 'I gave it another two bolts, but the dust was so thick then that I couldn't see what I was firing at. So I came back here.'

'What a blessing that we're all safe!' said Mrs Algeveer. 'Except poor Melinda,' she added hastily.

'Have you tried counting us?' Tim asked.

His voice sounded worried, so everyone tried counting. There was Mr and Mrs Algeveer, Tim, Sanchez, Karanda, Morween, Annomane, Jerk and the five cats. 'That was all. Of Sigmond, Barromane and the Uncle, there was no sign.'

'Where are the others?' asked Mr Algeveer wildly.
'They must have heard the blaster bolts going off.'

Just as he spoke there was a hiss of power from
outside and a flash of blue light came through the
windows colouring all their faces.

'It's the 4KO anti-grav making a very noisy take-
off,' said Tim. He was very good on engine noises
and had been exactly right about the blaster bolts.

'From the North Tower,' Annomane added.

Sigmond appeared on the balcony. He seemed to
have been running and he was much less confident
than usual.

'Barromane asked me to tell you,' he said, puffing
a little for breath, 'that he thought it was time he
brought the police in. So he's taken off for the Old
Capital.'

'And left us!' Mr Algeveer exclaimed. 'Didn't he
hear those blaster bolts and the cellars crumbling in
on my poor child's head.'

'What blaster bolts?' Sigmond asked. He looked
very blank.

'Is Uncle with you?' Sanchez suddenly
remembered.

'No, I haven't seen him. Isn't he with you?' Sigmond asked.

There was another of those awkward moments
when everyone looked suspiciously at everyone else
and the shadows of the rafters seemed to close in
even closer with their dragon masks and serpent
tails. The 3D portraits on the walls flickered and
scowled. Annomane ran her hand down a cat's back-
bone.

'We have lost him,' she said. 'I told you how important it was to choose rooms with the right auras.'

Of course, at that everyone began talking at once and Mrs Algeveer burst into tears. 'It's this terrible house,' she cried, 'it's closing in on us, taking us one by one.'

'It is very dark,' Tim said soothingly, 'and we don't really know our way around. I think that's why someone has got lost every time we've gone exploring. But now Barromane Barrouk has gone hurrying off to fetch the police.

'So we all might as well go to bed and get some sleep,' Karanda told them. 'When morning comes we'll have the police to help us and it will be easier in daylight.'

'She's right,' said Tim. 'But I suggest we sleep two to a room. Just in case. We don't want to lose anyone else.'

Everyone agreed, except Karanda, who said that she was quite capable of looking after herself. So Sigmond found a room for Mr and Mrs Algeveer with no spiders in it, and Tim and Sanchez went back to the room they had first liked – the one with the peaked rafters and the view of the falls.

They bolted the door carefully, searched all the cupboards and knocked on the walls to see if they were hollow. Everything seemed sound. The bed was suspended from the roof beams on four wrought-iron chains. It wobbled and shook as they got on to it, because Jerk insisted on lying at the end and the three Minims had to make a nest for themselves on one of the pillows. But when all six of them were settled it was beautifully comfortable. The bed clothes were scented with soothing herbs and the slight swing of the bed on its chains made them feel very sleepy.

'I won't say "Good night", said Sanchez, 'because I don't expect it will be a good night in this place. But it will be very nice to say "Good morning".'

Lulled by the soft rumble of the Falls of Dust they all fell asleep.

Chapter 7

In the deepest part of their sleep, in the very middle of the night, the bed began to climb up into the ceiling.

It went stealthily, inch by inch, and above the bed the ceiling rolled softly open to reveal a great dark hole. There was not a jolt to the bed or a squeal from the chains. Up and up it mounted until it was almost inside the dark hole.

It was Jerk who saved them.

Flying Hound Dogs never sleep deeply and he had been moaning and grumbling in his dreams for several minutes when a nasty nightmare about five flying cats woke him. For a second he looked about wondering what was wrong. Then he looked down and saw the floor ten feet away below him. With one frantic bound he leaped upon Sanchez and began licking his face.

'Warrat?' Sanchez murmured sleepily. The bed edged up another inch.

The Minims woke and began chittering to each other. Jerk put his paw on Tim's face.

'Hey!' said Tim. 'What's happening?'

'I'm all wet!' Sanchez sat up.

They both looked up at the dark hole just above them, then down at the faraway floor.

'Suffering stars!' Tim shouted. 'Scramble quickly and get out!'

Sanchez grabbed the three Minims; Tim pushed Jerk off the bed. The two boys sat for a moment on the edge as the whole bed tipped and swung. There was a sudden whirr of machinery as they jumped off and landed on the floor, stinging their feet with the impact. Even as they landed the bed shot up the last two feet and slammed into place.

When Sanchez looked up the bed had gone and the ceiling was complete again.

'Missed us!' he said.

'Only just,' said Tim.

'And thanks to Jerk,' said Sanchez, giving Jerk a hug. The Minims patted their fur back into place and made disapproving noises.

'Let's pick up our things quickly and get out of here,' said Tim. 'We'll get back to the dining-room, at least we'll be able to see around us there.'

The corridor outside had gone dark. A peal of distant thunder shook the Hall of the Falls of Dust as a storm approached. They groped their way along by the light of Tim's pocket torch. There were three passages, two flights of steps, several big cupboards and then another flight of steps. The thunder sounded again, much nearer this time.

'I don't remember this bit,' said Sanchez. 'The walls are very rough and the steps go on and on.'

'I think the dining-room will be at the end of them,' Tim replied hopefully. Jerk drew back whimpering and let them go first.

'It's a stone roof,' said Sanchez, 'and it should be wooden rafters!'

'Oh dear!' said Tim. 'I'm afraid we're in . . .'

'The cellar,' Sanchez finished for him.

The steps ended in a low vaulted hall. There was no furniture, but passages and doors opened out on every side. In the small pool of light from the torch the boys shuffled cautiously forward, on the alert for sudden drops.

A roll of thunder shook the Hall to the very foundations.

'At least we miss the lightning down here,' said Tim, shining his torch up and down.

'What's that?' Sanchez asked, knowing the answer before Tim replied.

Ahead of them, set in the wall, was a massive steel door. It looked very old and on each side of it was a tangle of ruined machinery, cogs and wires and switchboards.

'That must be the Second Transmitter,' said Tim. 'The one Ingar came out of.'

'All mixed up,' said Sanchez. 'It's the one he's supposed to haunt, isn't it? We don't have to hang around here, do we?'

'Look, there's where Karanda brought the roof down.' Tim pointed to a pile of broken stone and rubble. 'She said the lights of the Transmitter went on when she saw the ugly shape.'

'Well, they're off now,' said Sanchez, 'and by the look of that machinery they haven't been on for centuries. I'm cold. Let's get back upstairs.'

As he spoke two tall red lights went on, one

on each side of the Transmitter's steel doors. The lights were long bulbs held in the claws of stone gryphons.

'Golly!' said Sanchez. 'Now what's going to come out?'

There was the whine of machinery, almost drowned by another rumble of thunder. The whine went down the scale and stopped. Sanchez knew there were no such things as ghosts. At least he knew that Tim knew that. For himself he wasn't too sure. The idea of some monstrous figure from the past haunting the old Transmitter was upsetting. He wished Ingar's wife had smashed the Second Transmitter with her axe as well as the first.

They waited tensely. With a hiss the steel doors slid apart. And out stepped Karanda.

'Wow!' said Sanchez.

If Karanda was surprised to see them, she hid her feelings well.

'Wasn't it very dangerous to use a broken Transmitter?' Tim asked her. 'No one has ever made them work properly.'

'It's not a Transmitter, it's only an old lift,' Karanda reported casually. 'I got into it up in the North Tower. I didn't know it would end down here, but it explains several things that were puzzling.'

'Didn't you go to bed?' Sanchez asked.

'Would you go to bed and sleep if your uncle and aunt had been stolen away from you and an international gang of student elephants was trying to make a fool of your parents?' Karanda's eyes flashed angrily as she spoke.

'Do you think that is what is happening?' Tim looked serious.

'Of course it is,' Karanda snapped. 'And I'm not sure of you two either, so don't try any funny business. They've stolen my blaster, but I'm hot at unarmed combat.'

'Your blaster! How did they get that?' Tim asked.

'I threw it down on the table.'

'Yes, in a shredded fish salad. I saw it,' Sanchez butted in.

'I forgot to pick it up and when I went back it had gone. I'll bet Annomane took it. Wait till I catch up with her and her scratchy kitties,' Karanda breathed vengefully.

'You must have been hunting the place for ages,' Tim said.

'I have. I must have searched all five hundred rooms.' Karanda sounded a little tired behind her military manner, 'but I didn't find a trace of poor Uncle or Aunt. I found out one thing though. Barromane Barrouk is back – I came across his antigrav 4KO in the North Tower. I didn't see him, but I heard him laughing once, you know, like he does, ho! ho! ho!' Karanda imitated. 'But a long way off.'

'So he hasn't been for the police,' Tim said. 'He just sneaked back.'

'There is a very bad storm raging.' Karanda reminded them of the thunderclaps which kept rumbling away. 'He may have turned back because he was afraid to go on. In any case all the elephants
126

are here again and I'm going to find out what they're up to. Why are you down here for that matter?' Her eyes narrowed suspiciously.

They told her about their narrow escape with the rising bed.

'What!' she exploded, before they could finish their story. 'My father and mother had a bed like that in the room Sigmond found for them. Hurry! Follow me!'

They pounded after her, almost losing her as she shot upstairs and swung around corners. In no time at all they came to Mr and Mrs Algeveer's bedroom. Karanda didn't knock, she didn't even try the handle, she just brought a heavy stool down on the lock with a sideways chopping motion and smashed it. The door swung open.

'I knew it would be too late,' she said bitterly. The room was empty, even the bed had vanished. Karanda swung the stool up viciously to thump the ceiling. It rolled back to Tim's feet.

'Now what?' Karanda asked desperately. 'They've all gone except me. Where else can we look?'

'You didn't come across a library when you were searching, did you?' Tim asked her.

'A library, yes, there's a big one in the East Wing. What use is a library?'

'What we need is a plan of this place,' Tim explained. 'It's so rambling that we could easily miss parts of it, but a library is sure to have books about the place and they'll have plans. Cheer up, we're not beaten yet.'

'I'm never beaten,' Karanda looked firm again. 'Follow me, I'll show you.'

With never a hesitation, she led them up and down, through endless rooms and doors into a long, high room lined with bookcases. At the far end a full-length portrait in action 3D showed an old warrior squinting villainously and pulling a dagger from his belt. Sanchez looked up uneasily at this. Every time he moved the warrior pursed up his eyebrows and brandished his dagger; but it was only a painting.

'This'll be it,' Tim cried eagerly from the History section. ' "An account of the buildings of the Halls of the Falls of Dust in three volumes with", wait a minute,' his voice sounded even more excited, ' "with an appendix on its furnishings and invisibility banks." That's what we want!'

'Invisibility banks!' Even Karanda sounded lively now. 'Perhaps that's where they've been put. Quick! Get reading.'

'Aren't there any secret passages?' Sanchez was disappointed. 'What's an invisibility bank?'

'Much better,' Karanda assured him loftily. 'No one has used old-fashioned things like secret rooms and passages on this planet for a thousand years. They built invisibility banks instead. They're on the same principle as a force field. You can cut out a whole chunk of a room with gamma ion rays and step inside it and no one can see you, though you can see everyone. They have to be fitted, of course, and you have to know the key. There could be one up in the rafters of this room for all we know and Annomane could be sitting in it watching us.'

'Laughing at us!' said Sanchez.

'No, not laughing,' Karanda corrected him. 'The gamma ion rays cut out sight and you can tread on them, but they don't cut out sound waves so you have to be quiet. They were very useful in the old days when everyone was going around raiding and chopping off people's heads.'

'Got one!' Tim looked up from where he had been leafing through the third volume of his book. 'Here's an invisibility bank big enough for fifty people. It's in the big room where we had our dinner. This calls it the High Great Presence Chamber. The key to it is in a lion carving on the balcony. You activate the gamma ion rays and then just step into it.'

'Will it still be working?' Sanchez asked.

'Bring the book, we'll try that first.' Karanda was off already.

They followed her at breakneck speed down the long flight of steps through the entrance hall, then turned left into the room where Annomane had given them parched corn and water. Everything was dark now, but with two torches, Tim's and Karanda's, they made their way up to the balcony and found the carved lion. It had a fierce open mouth and a raised right paw.

'Place one finger upon the back of the lion's mouth,' Tim read out, 'then pull down its right paw. The invisibility bank will now be activated and you may step off the balcony without fear in a twenty-pace square, fifteen feet above floor level.'

'Karanda can step off first,' said Sanchez.

'One finger into its mouth,' Karanda repeated,

fiddling about with the lion's head, 'then down with its right paw.'

Sanchez heard the grating of the lion's paw. A curious crackling, fizzing noise ran through the great dark chamber, but there was nothing else, no light or sign of action.

'That should have done it,' Tim said doubtfully. 'I suppose we won't be able to feel the invisibility bank until we step into it ourselves.'

'I shall go first.' Karanda was as confident as ever. She scrambled up on to the rail of the balcony, hesitated a moment, then slipped off and disappeared into thin air. Even the light of her torch had vanished.

'It's worked,' said Tim happily. He jumped up and stepped out boldly. Then he too was gone and Sanchez was left in the dark.

'Come on,' he heard Karanda's voice calling from somewhere very close, 'and bring that dog. Quickly there's someone coming.'

Sanchez pulled Jerk over to the railings, picked him up and sat awkwardly balanced there. The Minims were safe in his coat pockets. It looked a long way down to the floor, but it was not as bad as stormriding at twenty thousand feet. Then he too heard voices and footsteps coming from the entrance hall. He stepped out into nothing and found he was treading on something firm but invisible just a few inches below him. At the same instant he could see Tim and Karanda again by their torchlight. They too were standing on nothing. Tim had a finger to his lips warning them to be quiet.

Carefully Sanchez stepped forward and found he was still firmly supported by the invisible gamma ion rays. Jerk did not like it. He pulled back and whimpered. Flying Hound Dogs expect to have to glide when they fall off balconies fifteen feet high. Sanchez cuddled him to try to keep him quiet, but he whimpered again.

'What is that noise? I can hear a dog somewhere. The poor creature is suffering. It must be helped.'

Looking down through the invisible floor Sanchez could see that Annomane had come into the room below. She pressed a hidden switch, flooding the room with silvery light. Barromane came in after her, tripping up over one of her cats. Sigmond and Morween were just behind him. All except Morween were heavily armed with two blasters apiece. Morween was carrying a small harp.

To Sanchez the view was extraordinary. Inside the invisibility bank he could see himself, Jerk, Tim and Karanda standing comfortably on what looked like thin air just above the heads of the four elephants. But it was clear from the way Annomane and Morween stared through them and around them that they were completely invisible from the floor.

The five cats had taken refuge on Annomane's shoulders and now they were spitting spitefully at Barromane for treading on them. Jerk whined again at the sight of his enemies and the cats looked straight up at him. Sanchez wondered if gamma ion rays were cat-proof.

'There,' Annomane boomed, 'I'm sure I heard

that dog again. See how watchful my kitties are. Seek him, Sketchybits! Seek, seek, Lillibits!'

Barromane stepped past her very awkwardly.

'It was nothing, cousin,' he said crossly, 'only the owls' call and the crickets' cry. You should keep your precious kittens on a tighter rein. I have suffered enough this night already.'

Then Sanchez noticed why he was stepping so awkwardly. The top part of his legs and the lower part of his body, everything he sat on in fact, was swathed in pads and bandages. In a side glance at Karanda, Sanchez saw that she was smiling triumphantly and making thumbs-up signs. Now they knew what she had hit with the three bolts from her blaster in the cellar.

'Sit down and rest, Cousin Barromane,' Annomane urged him. 'Take the weight off your legs.'

'I think not,' Barromane replied sharply. 'Until my paralysis has worn off it will be easier to stand! That wicked chit of a girl is still at large somewhere. We have the father, the mother, the uncle and the aunt, but our plan is incomplete until we have the girl as well. Where is she, Sigmond? She was your responsibility.'

'Morween lost her near the North Tower,' Sigmond reported sheepishly. 'She was hoping to lull her with sleepy music. Indeed I believe you played your harp outside a room for several minutes, didn't you, Morween?'

Morween lowered her eyes from the rafters and nodded gravely.

132

> *'Lap the ear in slumbers bright*
> *With fairy music of the night,'*

she quoted and played a delicate chord on the harp.

'Quite, quite,' said Barromane impatiently. 'But what was the result?'

'When my sister opened the door, she found that it was a lift shaft and empty,' Sigmond answered apologetically. 'The bird had flown!'

'Tcha!' Barromane snorted. 'At least we have her blaster. No one else will have to suffer my agonies. But she has probably joined forces with the two boys and we must abandon her. Time is not on our side. Listen, this is what we must do.

'We have four prisoners. With those in our hands as hostages we should soon have the A.U. Destructor and our triumph will be complete. Youth will have defeated Old Age. Ouch!'

Barromane staggered and tottered. One of the cats (Sanchez thought it was Naughtybits) had crept up around his feet and tripped him again. He would have fallen had not Sigmond and Annomane caught him. He groaned heavily.

'Kitties have as much right to living space as we have!' Annomane warned him. 'Remember we in the Youth Guild fight for a free galaxy for all living creatures including our dumb friends!'

'Miaow!' Naughtybits had climbed back on to her shoulder and was staring Barromane defiantly in the face.

Barromane controlled his temper with a deep sigh. 'Where was I?' he asked.

'You were saying that Youth had defeated Old Age,' Sigmond reminded him as they helped to prop him up against the wall.

'Ah yes,' Barromane went on. 'We can do without that wicked chit of a girl. If only we can get the other four safely off this planet, we will be able to demand any ransom we choose to name. So, we will leave the prisoners where they are. You, Sigmond, must drive the Sand Bat across the River of Dust as soon as the tide ceases to flow at dawn. You will tell the crew of our waiting anti-grav that we are ready. They will fly here, pick up the prisoners and take them to the space port before any alarm can be raised. At the space port there is an empty tourist liner waiting to fly off with us all. Within an hour at the very most we will have the prisoners safe on our secret asteroid and then we will be able to start dictating our own terms. The firm of Algeveer will learn that it is not wise to defy the inherited wisdom of us elephants. We of the Youth Guild will have saved civilisation from the menace of the A.U. Destructor.'

'What part remains for Morween and myself?' Annomane asked keenly.

'You two can pack and play the harp,' Barromane swung round scornfully. 'Aarh!' he cried as he made this unwise movement. He lurched back to the safety of the wall, shedding his heavy belt with its twin blasters.

'Perhaps a warm bath will give me some relief. I have borne the brunt of the day and hot water would be soothing.' He sighed again.

134

'Water!' Annomane snorted angrily. 'The spring deep below this house gives us two cups of pure water an hour and you talk of wallowing in a bath of it! You may have a warm dust bath any time you please, but nothing more.'

'Very well,' Barromane replied in a frail voice as he limped out of sight into the entrance hall. 'A dust bath will be better than nothing, if that is all I deserve.'

Sigmond and Morween exchanged glances and went out after him. Annomane was left alone with her cats. She was just bending down to pick up Barromane's blaster belt when Jerk whined again, long and low, almost a howl. Annomane spun round, gazed intently about the room, then cocked her head to one side. Just as Sanchez grabbed him, Jerk howled again. He was only about ten feet from Annomane and right above her head. The cats on her shoulders humped their backs and stared upwards. Sanchez was sure now that they could see through the gamma ion ray screen.

A broad happy smile spread across Annomane's face and she waved her trunk gracefully to the whole room.

'Ah the sweet voices of time!' she cried. 'I have heard the Spirits at last. Thank you, thank you for this. Come, my kitties, this is sacred ground.'

She dropped a stately curtsey to the empty far corner of the room and swept out, still smiling.

Jerk managed a last howl as Sanchez and Tim collapsed in helpless laughter on the invisible floor.

'You're a Spirit Hound!' Sanchez told Jerk.

'One of the sweet voices of time!' Tim spluttered.

Karanda stood tapping her feet on the floor that wasn't.

'All very well for you,' she said grimly, 'but those cunning elephants have got my family tied up somewhere, and if we don't act fast they'll have them away to their secret hideout on an asteroid and I'll be getting a letter with a ransom demand.'

'You're right.' Tim pulled himself together. 'We must help you to find them. They can't be far away from here.'

'But Jerk has done you one good turn,' Sanchez added. 'Look down there! Annomane was so excited when she thought she'd heard a real ghost hound that she forgot to pick up Barromane's belt. So we've got two blasters to defend ourselves with.'

Karanda's face lit up. She scrambled back quickly on to the balcony and down the stairs. The others followed after her.

'Great!' she said as she seized the belt and buckled it round her waist. 'It won't be on half power next time I use it!'

'It's no good starting a blaster battle with them,' Tim warned her. 'There are four of them already and Sigmond will be off at dawn across the river of dust to bring the rest of the gang in a big anti-grav. We don't know how far away they're lurking, but once he brings them back we're finished.'

'What we've got to do,' said Sanchez, 'is to find your parents and set up a defensive position somewhere in one of the towers. Karanda is a super shot and with these two blasters we should be able to hold the elephants at bay while one of us gets back to the Old Capital and brings *Dragonfall 5* and the police to the rescue.'

'That sounds fine,' said Tim, 'but Sigmond has the Sand Bat and Barromane is not so stupid as to leave the control keys lying about in his one-man 4KO anti-grav for us to fly away with it. So how do we get news back to the Old Capital. We can't walk!'

'Annomane has a jet-aided hang glider on top of the main tower,' said Karanda. 'I saw it when I was searching for Uncle and Aunt. It's only meant for a toy, but in this storm and with a west wind blowing you could risk a flight to the Old Capital. If you dared!'

She looked challengingly at the two brothers. Another tremendous roll of thunder shook the Hall.

'Well, that's an idea,' said Sanchez, who thought it was a very bad idea.

'Meanwhile,' said Tim, 'how do we find your family? Did you look everywhere?'

'Everywhere,' Karanda replied. 'I skimmed the whole place. They must be hidden away in some secret room like that invisibility bank. If only the elephants had mentioned it when they were talking.'

'Shall we creep after Annomane,' Sanchez suggested, 'and hope that she leads us there?'

'She's more likely to spend her time feeding spiders,' said Tim gloomily.

Jerk growled and swung round to face the door to the entrance hall. His big ears twitched and he scraped the floor nervously with one paw.

137

A cat was standing in the doorway watching them curiously.

'I think it's Naughtybits,' said Sanchez. 'He has a very pale head and he's the spiteful one that kept tripping Barromane up. It's a good job he can't talk or he'd go straight back to Annomane and tell tales about us. He's that sort of cat!'

'Hey!' Tim cried so excitedly that Naughtybits took a step backwards. 'Who says he can't talk? We've got the Minims and they can talk to anything. Minims!' he went on as the three furry animals popped their heads out of Sanchez's jacket pockets, 'you could talk to that cat there, couldn't you?'

The three Minims climbed up on to Sanchez's shoulder and inspected Naughtybits rather scornfully. Naughtybits had sat down in the doorway and was cleaning his fur.

'If necessary,' the first Minim said grudgingly.

'But cats are very narrow-minded animals,' said the second.

'Never mind that,' said Tim impatiently. 'What matters is that you can talk to him.'

'Why waste time with her horrid menagerie?' Karanda snapped crossly. 'It will be dawn in less than an hour. We've got better things to do than chat with cats!'

'But don't you see,' Tim explained, 'Annomane takes her cats everywhere so they'll know where your parents and your aunt and uncle are hidden!'

'That is a clever idea,' said Sanchez. 'I wish I'd thought of it!'

138

'Right!' said Karanda. 'Let's nobble the little brute.'

'Careful!' warned Sanchez. 'Even good-natured cats are very self-willed.'

'And no one would call Naughtybits good-natured,' said Tim. 'At all costs we mustn't upset him or he won't tell us a thing. I vote we leave him to Sanchez. He's good with animals.'

Tim took hold of Jerk so that there wouldn't be a fight. Then Sanchez walked forward very cautiously.

'Kitty, Kitty, Kitty, Kitty,' he called soothingly.

Naughtybits looked up from his bath, narrowed his eyes and watched Sanchez coldly.

'Come, Kitty, Kitty, Kitty!'

Very gently Sanchez crouched down and held his hand out towards Naughtybits.

Naughtybits sniffed the tips of his fingers for a moment then spat rudely.

'He's going to bolt,' hissed Karanda. 'I'll paralyse him with my blaster.'

'Wait,' Tim ordered her firmly. 'You're too handy with that blaster of yours. See where it's got you so far. Try patience for a change!'

Karanda scowled but said nothing.

Naughtybits had gone back to washing himself. He was bored with Sanchez's hand, but didn't mind the smell of it and didn't think it was dangerous. Sanchez put out his other hand and scooped Naughtybits up very carefully. For a second he felt a sharp pain as Naughtybits clenched all his claws into the arm that was carrying him. But Sanchez stroked him soothingly, right down from head to tail, and the claws relaxed. Sanchez continued stroking, a firm steady movement.

Naughtybits began to purr.

'Now, Minims,' Sanchez whispered. 'It's over to you. You know what we want this cat to tell us. Where are the prisoners and how do we get to them?'

'This is an exceptionally ill-natured cat,' said the first Minim.

'But we promise to do,' said the second.

'Our bit,' said the third.

For a minute the Minims inspected Naughtybits as he lay purring in Sanchez's arms, then they started to talk in cat language – a long string of miaows and hisses, wrigglings and throaty murmurings. As they began Naughtybits gave them a sidelong glance, then just lay back with his eyes shut. When they finished Naughtybits opened his mouth. He gave one low soft 'grrrh' sound, and jabbed his claws hard into Sanchez's arm.

Sanchez felt like thumping him but went on patiently stroking.

'Well, what did he say?' he asked the Minims.

'This cat,' said the first Minim.

'Wants to know,' continued the second.

'How much is it worth?' ended the third.

'Greedy wretch,' said Sanchez. 'But don't tell him I said that! Tim,' he turned to his brother, 'Gather up all the shredded fish salad that we left into one bowl and bring it here. Quickly please.'

Tim hurried around the table emptying the plates and ended up with a big bowl half full of oily fish bits. Cautiously he approached Sanchez and held the bowl out for the cat to see.

'Let him smell it,' said Sanchez.

Naughtybits opened one eye and looked casually at the bowl of fish. He shut the eye, lay back in Sanchez's arms and miaowed several times.

'This ignorant cat,' reported the first Minim, 'wants to try a piece of fish first to see if it is worth his valuable information.'

'Also,' said the second Minim apologetically, 'he wants you to start stroking him again.'

'And to scratch behind his left ear,' ended the third.

'Anything for a good cause,' said Sanchez, beginning the stroking and ear scratching, 'but only give him a very little bit of fish, Tim, so that he'll still be hungry.'

141

Tim offered Naughtybits a tiny piece of fish on the tip of a finger. Naughtybits ate it delicately and rubbed his whiskers. He miaowed again.

'He says he would like just one more piece before he tells you where the prisoners are hidden,' said the first Minim.

'But if we were you,' advised the second.

'We'd be firm and say "no",' ended the third.

'Take the bowl and stand in the door with it,' Sanchez told his brother. 'Now, Minims, tell this cat that if he doesn't start directing us to the prisoners this instant Tim will go out and throw the whole bowl of fish goodies into the river of dust. Make it sound very firm.'

The three Minims began to make the sort of noises that cats make before they start a fight: deep squawky noises down in the throat. As he listened Naughtybits dug his claws into Sanchez's sleeve, but Sanchez bore it and went on stroking. When the Minims had ended their speech, Naughtybits looked up once with slit-pupilled eyes at Sanchez, then miaowed and sprang lithely to the floor.

'He says follow me,' reported the Minims.

The pale grey cat padded to the door and passed Tim without a single upward glance.

'Tell him I'm behind him with two blasters if there's any funny business,' said Karanda.

Chapter 8

They set off in a strange procession up stairs and down corridors. First went Naughtybits, then Tim with the bowl of fish, then Karanda with a blaster in each hand and lastly Sanchez with his hand on Jerk's collar. The silvery lights had gone out and the dark passages were only lit by the blaze and flash of the lightning. They met no one, but as they groped and stumbled their way along, the muffled roar of the Falls of Dust began to smother even the great claps of thunder.

Finally they came to the foot of a staircase that wound up into the deeper darkness above them. Here the sound of the falling dust was deafening.

'This is the main tower,' Karanda shouted. 'I've been here. At the top of those stairs is the platform where Annomane keeps her hang glider. My parents aren't here, I've searched it all. That cat's cheating us!'

'They could be here,' Tim shouted back. 'You'd never hear them calling for help over all this noise. This tower must be built on the very edge of the falls.'

'Where is he going now?' Karanda pointed at Naughtybits who had jumped up on to a carved

143

stone face that peered out from the shadows under the stairs.

'He's licking his lips,' said Sanchez, 'so he must think he's due for his fish bits.'

Tim reached up and tugged at the stone head. Naughtybits sprang down on to his shoulder and bit at his ear, but Tim went on pulling. As he pulled, the whole inside wall of the stair swung forward on hinges to show a dark space behind. The noise of the falls grew even louder.

'What we want now is a good long flash of lightning,' said Sanchez, peering into the gloom.

The lightning came. For a few dazzling seconds, they could see down a short flight of steps into a wide chamber. Through the windows of the chamber the torrent of dust went roaring down, very close. But that was not what mattered.

Slumped asleep on couches and chairs were Mr and Mrs Algeveer, the Uncle and Aunt Melinda.

'Give Naughtybits his fish,' Sanchez shouted and cheered.

'Father!' cried Karanda; and then the lightning flash ended and they were left in the noisy dark once more.

'We've found them!' Sanchez shouted.

'I wish I could find my torch,' Tim shouted back. 'I've put my foot in the bowl of fish. Naughtybits has gone scatty!'

Karanda pulled a torch out of her space suit harness and shone its dying beam on to the corridor. It was true that Tim had trodden in the bowl of fish and the cat was leaping back in great bounds the way they had come. Then, by the flash of the next lightning, they saw why. Coming up the corridor, brandishing a blaster apiece, were Annomane and Barromane.

'We're trapped!' said Tim.

'Followed!' said Sanchez in dismay. 'Those cats probably never lose sight of each other. They just trailed us!'

'Stand back and make way for a professional!' Karanda snarled.

Without seeming to take aim she fired both blasters at full charge. The muzzles flared white hot. Two searing rays of light shot up to strike the ceiling of the corridor halfway between them and the two elephants. Instantly the heavy stone vaults collapsed with a crash that drowned both Falls and thunder claps. A pile of broken stone half filled the corridor and a swirl of dust billowed towards them. In front of the dust, moving even quicker, Naughtybits came leaping back to them to end up on Tim's shoulder again, spitting and arching crossly.

'That won't hold them long,' Karanda shouted, pointing to the barrier her blaster charges had created. 'They've got blasters too.'

Even as she spoke, the topmost stones of the new barrier glowed red and fell tumbling down as Annomane used her blaster on the other side.

Karanda fired again, only one shot this time, to let her second blaster recharge. Another length of ceiling came crashing down.

'This is great,' she turned laughing to the two boys, 'but it can't go on for ever. One of you has

145

got to get up this tower fast and take the hang glider back to *Dragonfall*. Who is it going to be?'

'Me!' said Tim and Sanchez both together. They paused and looked at each other.

'Really it had better be me,' said Sanchez. 'I can take Jerk. After all he is a Flying Hound Dog and they have a marvellous instinct for direction. He'll point the way home and I'll fly there.'

'Settled,' said Karanda crisply. 'Now go! We're

all here now in this tower and I can hold them off for ages.'

As she spoke she fired her second blaster on half charge at a stone that was falling from the top of the barrier. The stone flew over the other side and an angry shout came back.

'Use the rockets to give you a thousand foot height advantage and then the jet wind should carry you almost due east the way you want to go,' Karanda continued.

Sanchez saluted.

'Scramble!' he yelled. 'Come on Jerk!' and he was away up the staircase three steps at a time.

On top of the tower the full fury of the electric storm hit him. The lightning was almost continuous and the thunder claps never stopped. Annomane's hang glider was slung in a low shelter at the foot of a chute pointing up into the sky. Like most things belonging to Annomane it was very witchy, black, with wings cut to seem batlike. As he strapped himself into the harness, Sanchez looked at the controls. They were simple: speedometer, rocket firer, height indicator and the bar that worked the wing flaps. He had tried them out with the Algeveers on the evening they had sighted the phantom rocket ship, but this time there would be no safety reel to bring him back home automatically.

'Come on, Jerk,' he called. 'If Karanda is a professional we'll show her what amateurs can do!'

Jerk leaped up on to his lap eagerly. He loved anything to do with air travel. The Minims peeped out of Sanchez's pockets. They were never nervous but they did not like draughts. Sanchez fingered the rocket firing control. Karanda had said climb to a thousand feet to catch the jet stream. He knew that jet streams were strong air currents flowing like rivers in the upper atmosphere, but how strongly did they flow? Beneath him he felt the whole tower shake to three blaster bolts. They were at full charge so it was probably Karanda. There was no time to lose if there was to be anything left of the Hall of the Falls of Dust by the time he returned with *Dragonfall*.

He pressed the rocket firer at top power.

When *Dragonfall 5* took off she began slowly and then gained speed. The little hang glider shot away instantly, the thin pencil trails of her exhaust gases almost lost in a welter of lightning. Sanchez was dragged back in his harness and Jerk was almost torn from his arms by the pressure. The three Minims ducked down into his pockets, grumbling softly.

Up and up they soared into the night. Five hundred feet, eight hundred feet, one thousand feet.

Sanchez levelled off and cut back the rocket power. There would only be enough fuel in the small cylinders for half an hour's flying. Below him in the storm light he could see the long straggle of the Hall and beside it the lake of dust in its bowl of jagged rocks.

'Home, Jerk!' he whispered in the Flying Hound Dog's ear. 'Home, seek, seek, home, boy!'

Jerk turned his head confidently a little to the left and Sanchez wiggled the control bar in an easy turn to fly where Jerk was pointing. The bat wings billowed on each side of them in a surge of wind. It was the jet stream and it was blowing in almost exactly the right direction, due east. The speedometer wavered between eighty and one hundred and ten miles an hour; Sanchez realised that the flimsy glider was going almost as fast as the gusts that

149

carried it. He sat back in the harness hugging Jerk tightly because it was very cold. One of Jerk's big silky ears blew across his face like a warm scarf. It was almost enjoyable, but it would be nicer when it was over.

As the lightning dazzled and died Sanchez could make out a faint pink glow in the sky ahead of them. Surely not red lightning, he thought, then realised that it must be the dawn.

And with the dawn the river of dust would cease to flow and Sigmond would be free to drive the Sand Bat off to bring the rest of the gang. A hundred miles an hour was not enough. Sanchez corrected their flight direction to follow Jerk's nose and pressed the rocket firer again. With jet stream wind and chemical fire both doing their utmost the little glider hurtled on, its wings creaking and straining in the blast.

Most of the time Sanchez kept his eyes shut, only opening them every now and then to see which way Jerk was pointing. When the rocket fuel ran out their speed slackened to that of the jet wind. The sun was almost risen now and all the sky about him was a huge haze of geranium and rose, growing out of the darkness and washing it away. The storm was over.

'You're not going to sleep, Jerk, are you?' he asked anxiously as he noticed Jerk's nose drooping. Jerk snuffled as if to say 'what nonsense', and Sanchez realised that he was pointing downwards.

Below them, rising out of the desert sands, were the towers and pinnacles of the Old Capital and in the horseshoe shape of the city lay the space port where *Dragonfall 5* was berthed. They were back.

'You should be called Super Hound,' Sanchez told Jerk and swung the hang glider into a long downward curve.

Five minutes later he braced his legs to land running, and came stumbling to a stop hardly fifty yards from *Dragonfall 5*. Old Elias was frying bacon for breakfast and saw the little craft touch down. Sanchez put Jerk on his feet, unhitched himself from the harness and ran towards the old starship.

Still breathless and shivering from the flight, he poured out his story to his parents.

'Take-off will be in one minute, boy!' promised Old Elias as he vaulted into the pilot's seat.

'What about the police?' asked Sanchez. 'Shouldn't we contact them?'

'No time,' declared Old Elias cheerfully, 'and, with your mother on board, no need!'

As the trumpet clocks of the Old Capital were sounding the dawn hour in sweet clear music, *Dragonfall 5* blasted up over the wooden rooftops. The golden fire of her rocket engines challenged the dull crimsons of the sunrise as she raced back into the west. Big Mother was navigator, calculating their flight path, and Old Elias was pilot, pushing their rocket power to the top speed possible in low planetary flight. So they were back in seven and a half minutes.

As they came racing in over the desert on low trajectory, Sanchez spotted a large anti-grav ahead of

151

them. It was just coasting down for a landing on the slope below the castle.

'We're too late!' he called. 'Sigmond has brought up the rest of the gang. We can't land on a rocky slope like they can. They're going to get there first.'

'Say you don't know that if anyone asks you,' retorted Old Elias. 'Which is the tower our people are besieged in?'

'That one.' Sanchez pointed to the last tower of the Hall, the one overhanging the precipice where the Falls of Dust had roared in the night. Now in the red morning haze the Falls had stopped running.

'Right,' snapped Old Elias. 'Fasten your safety belts, we're going to make a tail landing right on top of that tower!'

Dragonfall roared up, steeper and steeper, in a climb until she was sitting on a column of blazing fire with her nose pointing straight up. All the cabin furnishings swung round on their gimbal fittings so that everyone was still sitting upright.

Carefully Old Elias manœuvred them until they were exactly above the tower. Then nine, seven, five, three, one, he reduced their rocket thrust so that they sank lower and lower to land tail first alongside the chute where Sanchez had taken off less than an hour ago.

Sanchez hurried to hang a long rope ladder down from the cabin door. Outside it was strangely quiet now that the Falls, the thunder and the blaster bolts were all silent.

Big Mother took a loudhailer with her as they climbed down to the tower. The roof was still
152

scorched and warm from the flame of their fast landing.

'Is it a truce?' Big Mother called down the stairs.

There was a short silence, then Barromane Barrouk's voice came feebly up to them.

'Yes, we will hold a parley before the castle walls.'

'But I must have Naughtybits back first,' Annomane's voice added much more confidently.

'Is that all right with you, Karanda?' Big Mother called down.

'The sooner she gets her horrid cat back the better we'll be pleased,' Karanda's voice came ringing up. 'But we must meet on their side of the barrier. We're not having them sneaking up on us.'

'Agreed?' shouted Big Mother.

'Agreed,' Barromane replied wearily. 'In my present unhappy condition I could not climb over the barrier even if I wished to.'

The *Dragonfall* party met Tim and the Algeveers at the foot of the stairs. All around them was the wreckage of the siege. Great holes were torn in the walls, dust billowing everywhere from the fallen ceiling. Karanda had a cut over her eye but she looked thoroughly cheerful. Mr Algeveer and the Uncle appeared very frail.

'Where are the police?' Tim asked, trying to control Naughtybits. 'How many of them have you brought? There's a new party of elephants just arrived with Sigmond.'

'No police!' said Old Elias.

'Why ever not?' gasped Mr Algeveer. 'We are outnumbered.'

'Well,' said Big Mother, 'once you bring the police in on a private quarrel it's very hard to end it.'

'But we don't want to end it,' Mrs Algeveer complained. 'We have been kidnapped and imprisoned and besieged by a gang of elephants. The sooner they end up in a law court the better!'

'Apparently,' said Big Mother slowly, 'your firm has invented a weapon, Algeveer's Universal Destructor, that can twitch a whole planet out of orbit.'

'That's true,' admitted Mr Algeveer. 'I invented it myself.'

'And these elephants, led by Sigmond and Mr Barrouk, are trying to get it away from you?'

'They were going to kidnap us and get the A.U. Destructor from my firm as a ransom. They are an intergalactic menace!' Mr Algeveer declared.

Big Mother pointed at the ruined corridor, the gaping walls, the fallen ceiling.

'This is what your daughter has done with two small pocket blasters,' she said seriously. 'Do you wonder that these elephants don't trust you with a weapon that can destroy whole planets?'

Karanda looked cross, Uncle Algeveer nodded, the other Algeveers were silent.

'So you see,' continued Big Mother, 'why I think it would be better for relations between humans and elephants if this quarrel were kept private.'

Mr Algeveer pursed his lips but still said nothing.

'Now let's climb over and talk to the other side,' said Big Mother. 'We're coming over!' she called.

They scrambled up over the heaps of shattered

stonework. On the other side, in a cloud of dust and blaster fume, Barromane was leaning limply on a pair of crutches. Annomane was still defiantly swinging a blaster. They had just been joined by Sigmond and a group of six young elephants. None of these had blasters and they all looked fresh and clean compared with everyone else. Morween was sitting in a window-seat apart from the rest. She was still carrying a harp and seemed more interested in the colours of the sunrise than the truce.

'Well?' said Big Mother.

'No, I am not well,' said Barromane faintly.

'How do we stand?' Big Mother turned to Sigmond, who smiled politely.

'You can't beat us,' said Sigmond, 'and we can't beat you.'

'That's what I thought,' Big Mother agreed.

'You could get us all into bad trouble with the police if you got away from here,' Sigmond went on. 'But we could make it very difficult for you to leave here. A few blaster bolts on your rocket pods, you know?'

'We know,' said Big Mother. 'That's why we called a truce.'

'We want the A.U. Destructor,' Sigmond declared firmly, 'and we're going to have it. Humans are not safe with powerful weapons.'

'Just exactly who are you all?' Mr Algeveer asked.

Barromane swung wearily on his crutches.

'I lead the Youth Guild,' he said, and coughed. 'We are a group of actors and artists interested in racial harmony.'

'And I represent Students for Peace,' Sigmond reported briskly. 'Our two organisations decided that the firm of Algeveer was becoming a menace to racial harmony and peace, so we have united to control it.'

'So all the bad things that have plagued me on this holiday were your doing?' Mr Algeveer asked plaintively.

'Yes,' said Sigmond, 'though superstitious people are very easy to frighten.'

'You arranged the phantom space ship, did you?' Tim asked. 'How was it managed?'

'That was my doing,' Barromane perked up a little. 'Used as I am to projecting the images of actors millions of miles across space, it was simplicity itself to project a reel of an old space film a mere five miles into air from one of the towers of this Hall. So you thought you saw Chutar's Ride. It was well done, though I say it myself, and of course Mother Morrow's flames in the sky were even easier to arrange. She herself is one of our best actresses.'

'I suppose,' said Mr Algeveer, 'that if I were to promise you that I'd never develop the A.U. Destructor, that wouldn't satisfy you?'

Sigmond turned to the other young elephants. They all shook their heads.

'I thought not,' said Mr Algeveer, 'so my brother has another idea which may please you more.'

Everyone turned hopefully to Uncle Algeveer who took a large envelope from his pocket.

'Our firm,' the Uncle began, 'has the secret plans by which the A.U. Destructor can be made. No one else has these plans, so no one else can make it. You understand?'

Everyone nodded.

'But in this envelope is a legal agreement by which the only people allowed to manufacture the A.U. Destructor are . . ., and there we have left a blank space in which I propose to write "The Youth Guild" and "Students for Peace".'

'But we could not manufacture it because we haven't got the secret plans,' Barromane protested.

'Exactly,' said the Uncle, 'and though we will have the secret plans we could not manufacture it because we will have given you the only legal right to make it.'

'So nobody will be able to make it!' Sigmond was smiling. 'If you try to make it, we could take you to court and stop you.'

'A very happy arrangement, I think,' said the Uncle, 'and if you would care to fill in these blank spaces, we can end our private war with no real losses.'

'Except my back.' Barromane glared at Karanda.

'People who play at ghosts in dark cellars get what they deserve,' said Karanda, 'and my blaster was only at half-power!'

Using a windowsill as a table, they filled in the blank spaces of the Uncle's legal document. Sigmond kept one copy and the Algeveers kept the other. While this was going on, Naughtybits slunk around looking very unsure of himself. At first Annomane pretended to ignore him, but she could not keep that up for long. She pounced on him and

157

swept him up in her arms, hugging and kissing him fiercely while he miaowed and miawled in protest.

'Did they tempt my precious away from mother then?' she said with a glare at Tim who had been holding him.

Tim and Sanchez exchanged looks but said nothing.

'Now that's settled,' said Sigmond, folding away his copy of the agreement, 'and our twin planets can go on happily together with the humans doing the hard work and the elephants making sure they don't work too hard for their own good. I think my sister has a poem for the occasion.'

Morween stood up in a faint ray of pink sunshine and struck three low chords on her harp.

'Elephants and humans must agree
To guard all weapons sensibly.
Through storm and stress and violent weather
Our races both must live together,'

she sang, then smiled very sweetly at everyone.

People were just about to clap politely when Karanda spoke.

'In case you think that only elephant girls can write poetry,' she said, 'I've composed a few lines myself. This is how they go:

'When blasters make you duck and dive
I think it's great to be alive.
Perhaps it's time now for a rest
Yet battle really is the best.
We'll sign our peace and go our ways
But fight like mad some later days.'

158

'How's that?'

She looked around defiantly.

'Well, dear . . .' Mr Algeveer began. There was an awkward pause. It was broken by a long cross miaow from Naughtybits.

'What does petal want to say?' Annomane asked, cuddling him tightly. 'Has petal written a poem as well as the naughty people?'

'Actually,' said the first Minim, popping his head out of Sanchez's top pocket.

'He wants to know,' said the second Minim.

'When he's going to get that bowl of fish he was promised!' ended the third.

BRIAN EARNSHAW

DRAGONFALL 5 BOOKS

If you have enjoyed this Dragonfall book, you will want to read about all the other comic adventures on board the Dragonfall 5 with Tim, Sanchez, Old Elias and Big Mother, not to mention Flying Hound Dog Jerk and the inquisitive Minims.

There are six other Dragonfall books.

Dragonfall 5 and the Royal Beast
Dragonfall 5 and the Hijackers
Dragonfall 5 and the Space Cowboys
Dragonfall 5 and the Empty Planet
Dragonfall 5 and the Super Horse
Dragonfall 5 and the Master Mind